THE UNICORN PRINCESS

THE PACIFIC PRINCESSES BOOK 1

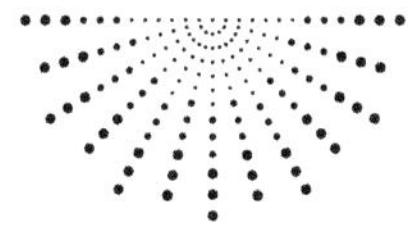

EKTAA BALI

BLUE MOON RISING PUBLISHING

ISBN: ebook: 978-0-6489830-2-6

Print: 978-0-6489830-3-3

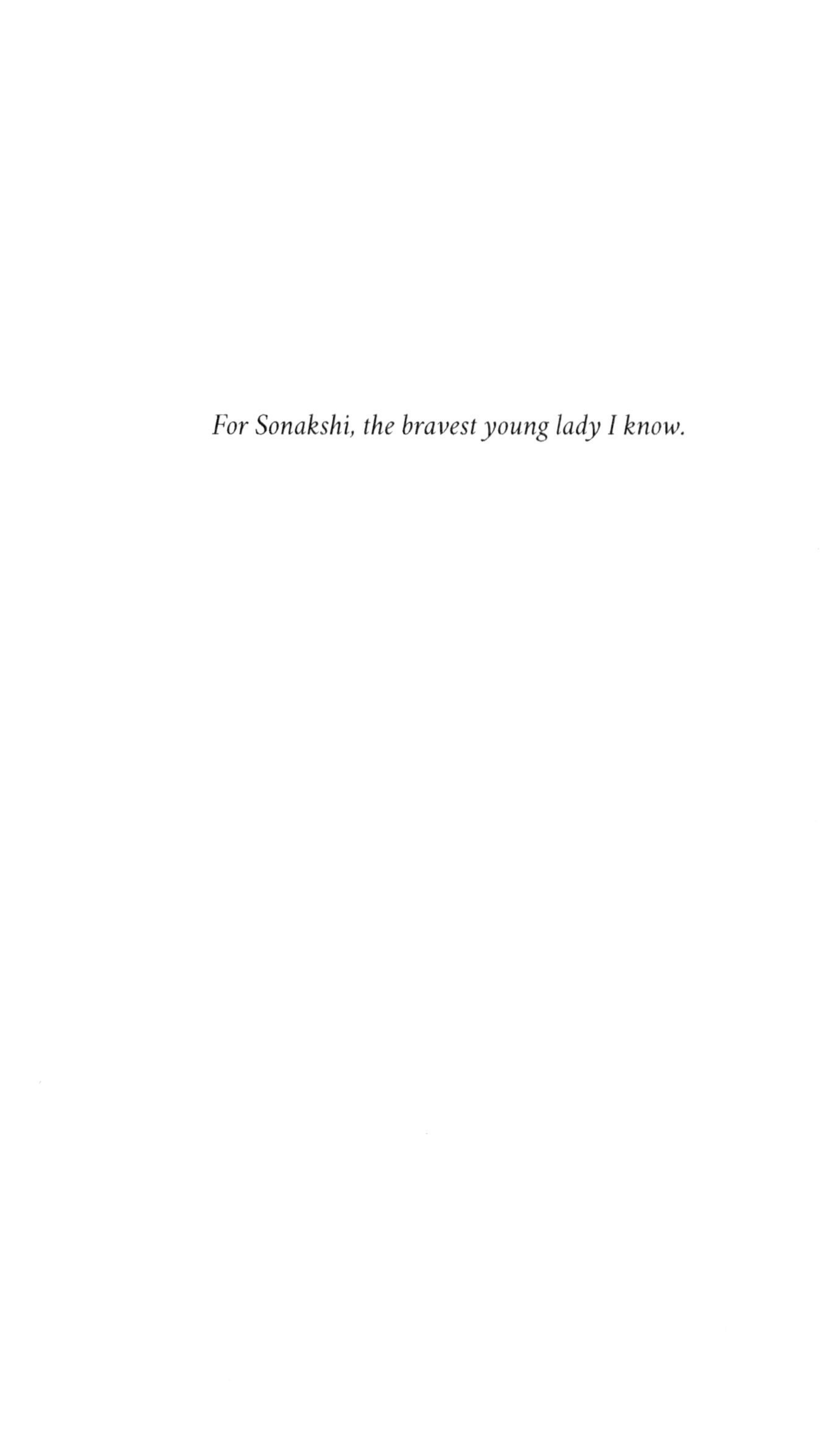

For Sonakshi, the bravest young lady I know.

THE UNICORN PRINCESS

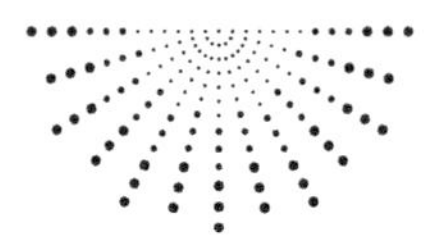

In the far and lonely parts of world, trod creatures with secrets. They can be sly and wise, fair and dark, noble and ignoble. They are not for the eyes of men, who taint the very air with mundane thoughts and mundane actions. Regardless, the human eye could not do justice to these creatures, for it was made to see fear over love and the mundane over the profound. But every so often, these creatures make themselves known to people. They emerge from the wilderness out of great curiosity or even greater love. One such creature known to do this is the Unicorn, the purest and most powerful of them all. But one should pause to consider the enormity of such a decision. It is a sacrifice, a gift, and an honour to know a unicorn. There are those who would take such a gift and twist it in their cold dark hands, for even colder, darker purposes.

-Lord Anthony Godfrey, *The Annals of Unicorn Sightings in the 16th Century, 1701.*

PROLOGUE

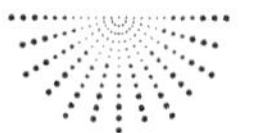

The thunder roared and flashes of bright lightning illuminated the sky over Suva harbour at midnight, as the royal couple sprinted down the road, clutching onto one another's hands. They ran against the battering of the rain, and against the onslaught of time—and it even felt to them as if they ran against the assault of the entire world.

The childling lying swaddled in the Queen's arms cowered, squeezing close into her mother as if she might, with just some luck, return into the womb where she had found it safe and warm just three years ago.

The white lightning lit up the harbour again, and they caught sight of hundreds of masts swaying like obscene, dancing jesters in the swelling ocean.

"Almost there," yelled the child's father, the King, over the beating of the rain. "Hold—"

He was interrupted by a furious, terrifying scream of such anger and grief that it made the group of three stumble. The Queen herself screamed too, frightful yet gentle in comparison, before pressing on, clutching her daughter even more tightly. The King followed, and they pelted down the jetty, desperately hoping their furious pursuer had not realised their motive.

A purple-sailed boat stood proudly amongst the other yachts which danced aggressively in the water. Its most pronounced feature was that it seemed not to be moving at all; instead, the vessel sat as still and patient as the blue-bearded man who held onto her anchor with powerful arms.

"Come on! Into the cabin below!" he called, against the rain, and they ran past him, straight onto the boat.

King Farrion of the eastern bushland fae strode on after them as another howl of anger sounded across the jetty, much closer this time. His expression was serious.

He stroked his blue beard as he strode to the wheel of the *Dancing Dimple*. "Onwards!" he commanded. "With all the speed of the fae behind you, we shall head west across the Pacific!"

The purple sails billowed out as the wheel of the yacht spun fast of its own accord, and the *Dancing Dimple* launched herself with full speed across the incensed, swirling black ocean.

Feeling his neck prickle, Farrion turned to look back at the harbour as they left it behind. The lightning was not yet relenting, and it flashed across the jetty, revealing the shape of a hunched woman whose face was so disfigured it barely looked like a face at all.

She shook her fist at Farrion, speaking words that he was grateful were lost to the storm.

She shrank as the *Dimple* sped out farther into the ocean, and shaking his head, he descended the wooden stairs to the cabin below, his heavy boots clomping on the narrow wooden steps. He did not have to call out to forewarn of his arrival down below, since the vibration and noise of his footsteps overshadowed even the wind and rain.

The King and Queen of Macuata were shivering, drying themselves with towels.

"How long will it take?" asked the Queen anxiously, sitting on the edge of the bed, unravelling her small daughter from the bundle of blankets in front of her.

And for the first time in two hundred years, the heart of the Fae King skipped a beat. This was no ordinary child.

He knew precisely what she was, but to see her true form with his own eyes was a different matter entirely.

On the bed before him lay a tiny, delicate foal that shone with the light of the moon. She was so small that she had been easily concealed in her mother's arms.

A jewelled horn sparkled from her forehead and small, brilliantly feathered wings were tucked tightly to her side. She trembled on delicate legs as her mother gently towelled her down, wiping the dripping water from her shiny mane. Her eyes shone a brilliant gold, like pools of molten metal. *Those eyes*, the King thought, *will forever mark her for what she is.*

"Shh," whispered the Queen, pulling the unicorn foal towards her.

"It's alright, you can turn back now." Before his eyes, the foal erupted with gold light, and when it dimmed, there sat a little dark-haired girl no older than three, her delicate skin the colour of pure honey, just like that of her parents. The tiny, beautiful unicorn foal had disappeared.

The only things that remained to mark her out were her golden-coloured eyes.

"Sonakshi," cooed the Queen. "Let's put this jumper on you."

The King almost laughed, since *Sonakshi* meant 'golden-eyed one' in Hindi.

It took the Fae King a second to realise he had not answered her question from a minute earlier: how long would the journey take?

"Ah the voyage…" King Farrion said, "Well, in this fae vessel, from Fiji to Australia should take around two days, Your Majesty."

"Oh please," she replied, graciously. "I will not have the King of the Fae addressing me so. It's Ria. You must know that Devin and I are *incredibly* grateful for your help."

Having roughly dried his hair, Devin came over to Farrion and grasped his hand warmly.

"I can't believe you came to our assistance so quickly. Had we known about the witch, we would have called for your aid sooner."

Farrion took a seat at the kitchen table, smiling kindly at the child before him, now swamped by a large red woollen jumper.

“These things happen. Now you are cousins of ours, in a way.”

Devin took a seat on the edge of the bed opposite Farrion, leaning forward eagerly.

“Did you find out anything?”

Farrion nodded, his face serious again.

“She is the only one.”

He was met by stunned silence.

“She is… Are you sure?” whispered Ria, pulling her daughter to her chest.

She had come dangerously close to losing Sonakshi tonight, and she needed to be sure of exactly how much danger she was in. “The only one?”

“Quite. The eastern fae know of no other unicorns in our part of the world.”

Devin clapped his hands together, once.

“Well. We will just have to keep her a secret. Others will come after her, surely,” he said.

Farrion nodded slowly. A secret she would have to be, then.

His people understood secrets; in fact. they might very well have invented the word.

“But wasn’t there ever another in the family? She cannot be the first one,” he asked.

Ria and Devin exchanged a knowing look.

“My great grandfather,” said Ria. “It comes from him.”

Farrion nodded, standing up. He smiled and cast his hand around, as if to say, *make yourselves at home here.*

“Settle down for the night.” He said. “You are safe on the open ocean with me.”

Princess Sonakshi listened to the adults talk with the wide-eyed wonder of a three-year-old.

She might not have understood the meaning of most of the words they spoke, but she smelled the fear in the cabin as surely as she smelled the stew cooking on the tiny kitchen stove.

She also knew she was scared, and hungry, and cold, despite the thick blanket her mother insisted on wrapping around her each time the wind would come whistling through tha cabin again.

For all the days in the rest of her life, she would remember that sharp smell of fear in the cabin. It was the urgent, all-consuming need to flee, to hide, to run, to be safe.

True to the King's word, they reached the shore of Freshwater Bay, on Australia's Eastern Central Coast, two days later, arriving in the dark of midnight; the moon and stars were their only audience. This land smelled different. Gone were the tall coconut trees and heavy density of a wet climate. Here, the air was crisp, dry, and clean. And the birds—Sonakshi turned her wide, golden eyes up to the trees—the birds here, *laughed.*

They travelled through the bushland for a day and a half with Sonakshi secured safely to her father's back, and they headed through a mountain pass into a deep valley.

Men below, armed with spears, cut and hammered wood next to a small cabin.

"The Blue Mountains," Farrion said. "So remote, no one will ever come upon you. I have arranged for guards and a shelter until you can build your own, in time."

He nodded to Devin, who was skilled in engineering.

"Pay them with gold and kindness and they will never betray you."

"Who is that?" asked Devin as he pointed to a tall, pale, red-headed man on a hill, gesturing to the men with one hand and holding a small child on his hip with the other.

"A great friend. Lord Oscar of Cabbage Tree Creek. He is going to be your only neighbour for a hundred miles."

Sonakshi tugged at her mother's sleeve.

"Mumma, are we safe now?" she whispered.

The Queen took her daughter and sat her down on a moss-covered rock.

"This our new home and we will work hard to keep harm away from you. You are a rare thing, my love. Both cherished and coveted by all."

And the unicorn princess heard her mother's words. But in the tremble of her voice and the heated gaze within her eyes, she felt her mother say, *you will never be safe*.

CHAPTER ONE

Unicorns are the natural secret keepers of the universe. They understand the hidden things that move the world, they understand the hidden paths that must be walked, but most of all, they understand the secrets we keep in our hearts, for they are most precious and troubling of them all.

Lord Anthony Godfrey, *The Annals of Unicorn Sightings in the 16th Century*, 1701.

Seven years later

It was midday in the Blue Mountains, and deep in the bushland, in a hidden valley well away from the rest of the world, lay a peculiar group of buildings.

On one side of the valley lay several quaint wooden cottages housing the guards who protected the area, and all their wives and children.

On the opposite side of the valley sat rows and rows of fruits, vegetables, and herds of cows, goats, and sheep, enough to sustain the small community.

Mostly notably, in the center of the valley was a spectacular three-story sprawling complex created of stone and wood. Everyone who lived there called this place *the castle.*

It had a central building, with large wings branching off all sides and strong turrets on each of its four corners, a rather well-planned feature. The man who had designed it had a particular knack for building large structures, and now, living so remotely, he had nothing better to do than dedicate his life to building a home for his little family and the people guarding them.

For six years, he and his men had toiled, pulling stone, and cutting wood to build the strongest structure out of the precious raw materials they had, maximizing local resources.

They fortified each wall a number of times, limiting the entrances on the ground floor to four, each always secured by a guard or even two. One could not but help get the feeling that anybody building such a thing was protecting something.

Or hiding something.

Or keeping something a secret.

And in this case, all three of these things were true.

* * *

A bright sun beat down upon the castle as Sonakshi and her best friend Kiera ducked behind a hay bale. "Phew," Kiera said, pushing her red hair off her pale-as-milk face.

The sun made her freckles stand out even more.

Sonakshi snuck a look around the hay bale, her black hair swinging.

Under the shade, their tutor, Dame Marie Norton, droned on, drawing on the blackboard while the other children sat at their desks, fighting sleep. Someone had mistakenly thought the children would pay more attention if they studied outside, enjoying the sunshine and breeze.

"The Yowie is a mythical bushland creature, almost impossible to find..."

She was drawing a picture of a large ape-like creature, with long, thick arms.

Off to the side, Captain Sampson was picking at his fingernails while Laurie and Andrew remained engrossed in their card game.

The two girls—Kiera and Sonakshi—had easily slipped away, unnoticed.

"Ok," Sonakshi whispered, turning. "Let's—"

"Hey guys!"

They both groaned as Rowen popped his round face around the other side of the bale.

With flaming hair and the same pale skin scattered with sun spots, Kiera and Rowen were unmistakably siblings and very much Irish.

"Shh!" Sonakshi grabbed Rowen around his chubby waist and pulled him into the shadow of the hay bale. His eyes widened as he realised they were hiding.

"Oh," he whispered.

"What are you doing?" whispered Rowen.

"Mind your own business, froggy." She ruffled his hair roughly.

"You can't just leave me behind!" he protested. "That's not fair!"

"Go back to class!" Sonakshi hissed.

He pouted, and Kiera scoffed at him. "Seriously!"

"Look you're going to give us away again," said Sonakshi, irritated. "Can't you just go somewhere else, please? And don't tell anyone you saw us. You always follow us *everywhere*."

The corners of his mouth turned down and his lower lip trembled.

"Come on, you're almost eight," Kiera said. "Go back to Dame Marie!"

But Rowen ignored her, his green eyes lighting up at Sonakshi instead.

"Sonakshi, are you going to practice flying again?" he asked her. His eyes glistened as he stared at her keenly. "I want to see the unicorn!"

Kiera groaned, but Sonakshi felt sorry for him.

He always cheered in delight when he saw her change into her other self.

"Oh, alright then."

"Yay!" he squealed, but Kiera threw him a dirty look before turning to Sonakshi and saying, "What did you agree to do that for? We were already playing..."

She scowled and sounded envious, not wanting her brother to keep interrupting like this.

But Rowen came around to Sonakshi and hugged her around the shoulders vigorously.

She hastily shushed him again.

"Okay, but we have to be quick," Kiera said. "Sona's prison guards will notice soon,"

"They're not my prison guards!"

Kiera made googly eyes at her best friend as they bent low and ran around the castle to the back lawn, where all the giant pumpkins grew. They could have a few moments there in secret, as everyone was usually busy out the front, and the giant vegetables and their leaves provided cover to hide behind. Dame Marie hardly ever noticed if Sonakshi went missing anyway, since she was always engrossed in whatever lesson she had for them that day.

That was why Captain Sampson, or one of the other guards, had to be around at all times.

Behind the castle, down near the pumpkin patch, was a nice long strip of green grass that Sonakshi had been using, in secret, as a runway.

Kiera ran forward and placed a small pumpkin halfway down the strip.

This was Sonakshi's marker, her point of takeoff.

Sonakshi placed herself at the end of the lawn—and did one of her most favourite things in the world. As she closed her eyes, she was enveloped with light, beginning to change shape completely, becoming longer and stronger. Steel hooves grew from her hands and feet, and fine silver hair covered her body, shimmering with her own light.

Wings made of beautiful opalescent feathers stretched outwards and then folded down by her sides, softly and silently. And finally, from her forehead grew a shiny horn made of glittering diamond. Her horn caught the light of the sun and reflected it so brilliantly that Rowen and Kiera couldn't help but gasp in awe. No matter how many times they had seen her change forms over the years, the sight of something so wondrous and magical never got old.

Sonakshi eyed the pumpkin and took a deep breath. She launched forward at a canter, then a full gallop, shining hooves kicking up the clouds of dust and dirt behind her.

She heard Rowen clapping excitedly as she stretched out her wings on either side of herself, feeling the air moving against them, giving her lift. She reached the pumpkin and brought her wings down hard, leaping into the air at the same time. She swooped her wings down, once, twice... and then fell straight down onto the grass with a painful thud.

"Ow!" she cried, landing on her front legs.

In truth, it didn't really hurt to fall.

She had never ever truly injured herself or even bled.

The *ow* came more from the shock of the whole thing, and from the embarrassment of being seen. But also, the pain of not being able to get any higher in the sky than the day before hurt more than anything else.

Kiera and Rowen ran towards her as she shook herself off, grumbling.

A shout made her look up.

There, having clearly just rounded the castle corner, sporting very unhappy looks on their faces, were her mother, father, Captain Sampson, Tammy—Rowen's nanny—and Dame Marie and some of their classmates, all pointing and giggling.

Her father angrily pointed at the door, his lips set into a grim line.

"Inside. Now!"

Sonakshi's heart fell as she hastily changed back into her human form, her heart thumping in her chest. They would have seen her fall. In fact, *everybody* would have seen her fall.

And everybody had seen her *fail* yet again.

She walked with her head down towards the back entrance of the castle, thoroughly embarrassed. Kiera and Rowen made to follow her, but Tammy came forward and whisked them away back to Dame Marie, whispering angrily at the pair.

Sonakshi felt her parents enter the castle behind her.

It was cool inside, but that did not help the heat burning in her face.

Now, she buzzed all over with the shame and adrenaline of it all, and as if that weren't bad enough, her parents were going to give her a scolding yet again. They always did, every time.

Her father moved in front of her and led them to the dining hall, currently empty before the ladies served lunch. She took a seat and waited, not meeting their eyes as they sat opposite her.

"Sona, you could have gotten really injured trying that stunt again. We don't know what on earth you think you are doing; we specifically told you not to fly."

Her mother had beautiful brown eyes and an oval, honey coloured face.

Sonakshi knew she looked like her mother, and that must have been why she always found it so hard to look at her every time she was being told off. She had let her mother down again.

"I'm sorry," was all she could say, not sure if it was actually true, though.

She was still buzzing from the energy of her gallop and felt her veins sizzling.

Her mother gave a long sigh, clasping her hands together and wringing them, irritated.

"I know you want to—"

"No, you don't know," said Sonakshi, heat rising up inside her. "You don't know what it's like at all! Because it's not like that for you!"

"Mind your tone, young lady," said her father, coal-black eyes glittering in warning.

Sonakshi stared at her lap, pursing her lips, feeling as though she was going to explode. But it was true though; they knew *nothing* about being her. No one did. They didn't know any other unicorns, and maybe there just weren't any more to be found. So how *could* they know?

How could they possibly understand how she felt useless and powerless being something that everyone envied and admired, when she really couldn't do anything at all? She was never allowed to just be herself, to just be silly, to let go of everything—and simply fly.

"Everything we do around you, Sonakshi, is for

your safety," said her father. "I need you to listen to the rules around here. No more flying. You understand me. young lady?"

"No more being a unicorn either?" she grumbled.

"Pardon?"

Her father's dangerous tone cooled her immediately. "Nothing."

They shifted uncomfortably in their chairs.

"You could have really hurt yourself, my love," said her mother gently. "If you hurt your leg or your hoof, we wouldn't know how to fix it. We don't know any unicorn doctors."

Her dad cleared his throat.

"Fine. No flying," she said flatly.

Although, she thought miserably, *I never really flew. And at this rate, I never will.*

She felt like bursting into tears.

But a loud CRASH sounded from behind her. In shock, adrenaline coursing through her, Sonakshi flashed into her unicorn self, spinning around to see the source of the huge commotion. Her parents jumped up to find one of the ladies from the kitchen had dropped two large, empty pans in the hallway. She quickly picked them up, calling out an apology.

Sonakshi grimaced and turned back to her human self.

It was lucky her clothes always managed to return to her when she changed back into a human, even though they bizarrely disappeared whenever she became a unicorn. It was lucky because every time something frightened her, she involuntarily turned into her unicorn self.

If the clothes never reappeared, she would be going through wardrobes and wardrobes of them. They all sat down, sighing, and her father drummed his fingers on the table top.

"This is why you can't leave the valley with us," said her mother sternly. "If you lose control like that in front of the members of the public, people will have all sorts of reactions and soon, we'll have them coming and wanting to test your blood, or your tears—"

"Why would they want to test my tears? And besides, you told me there are others like me. So, I'm not that interesting—"

"*Like* you, perhaps. But not the same as you, Sona. I mean there are merpeople, and the fae and their distant cousins, but just not the *same* as you. I keep saying, you're the only one."

Sonakshi sighed and rubbed her arms as if she was cold all of a sudden.

She just wanted to go back to Dame Marie's class out in the sun and be with Kiera, laughing at a guard picking his nose or something.

"We are reminding you of this," mother said, "because we are leaving for a trip in two days. You must start behaving, Sona. Promise me, you won't keep changing into your unicorn form."

"But I don't even plan it, Mother," said Sonakshi, somewhat indignant. "You know the loud noises set me off, stuff like that… I can't help it."

"Yes, I know that. But if you indulged it less, maybe

that would also stop it happening. Attempting to fly whenever we aren't looking maybe makes it easier to just slip into being a unicorn whenever you're scared. I don't know but—just stop trying to fly, ok?"

Sonakshi jerked her head up to look at them both.

She was no longer even listening properly. Now, she was no longer thinking about the flying or about how sudden noises made her turn into the strange little horse, but she was wondering why they were leaving to go off someplace all of a sudden?

They had never, not in the seven whole years they had been in the valley, left to go somewhere else, due to all the reasons they were always arguing about—and more.

"We're going on a trip?" she said excitedly. Kiera and Rowen went on trips all the time. Last year, they had gone to the Swiss alps, and next year, it would be Dublin.

"No," Father said, carefully. "Just your mother and I are going. We need to go to the annual conference in Sydney. It's about time we attended. Now you are older, that is."

Sonakshi just gaped at them, her mouth hanging open.

"You're leaving me *here?*"

Her mother took her hand and stroked the back of it with her soft, warm fingers.

"Seven years is a long time for us to be cooped up in here, but we think it's a bit early for you. Kiera and Rowen will stay here too, as their parents will be coming with us."

She should have known her parents would never take her anywhere.

It would have been so nice to go out and see a different place, even just a little. But as they always said—over and over—it was way too risky for her to travel.

There were untold dangers out in the world. She had even met one of those dangers once, when she was a baby. She couldn't remember it well, but her parents told her the story until it felt like a recording stuck inside her head. Nope, no travel. It would be heaps safer and easier if she stayed where she was until she was *much* older and had more control.

Besides, they had everything they needed here in the valley. And the thought of herself and Kiera, alone in the castle without their parents?

Well, they were going to get away with *so* much.

This was going to be great!

CHAPTER TWO

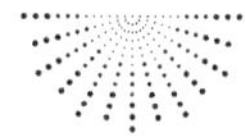

Unicorns do not forget a face. Though a human may wither and grow old, a unicorn will always remember you. I saw a unicorn when I was a boy, and I hunted for him for the rest of my life. I met him again as an old man in a different time and place. And he knew me. Right to my very bones, I knew it. I could see it in his eyes.
—Lord Anthony Godfrey, *The Annals of Unicorn Sightings of the 16th Century, 1701.*

It was midnight in the Blue Mountains and Sonakshi shook Kiera awake.

"What?"

"Wake up you dingbat, we're going on a hunt!"

It was the night before their parents were scheduled to leave for Sydney, so, of course, the girls had planned a daring mission for that very night. They had seen Ava, the head cook, receive a delivery of chocolates, among other things, and being such a rarity, they had to get their hands on some. They could grow and make plenty of things in the Valley, but chocolate was not one of them. Sonakshi's pile of food hidden under her bed grew weekly.

They, especially Kiera, found they were always hungry in the middle of the night and forbidden to go into the kitchens. So, naturally, they had learnt from a very young age to sneak around the castle under the cover of darkness and break into the kitchen.

The girls put on their dressing gowns and crept up to Sona's bedroom door.

"Willie Wagtail is leaving the nest. I repeat, Willie Wagtail is leaving the nest."

Kiera ducked out of Sonakshi's room and down the hallway.

Sonakshi checked the hallway left and right. It was dark, lit only by the lanterns lining the walls. She could hear Tammy snoring loudly in the room next door.

Two doors down was the room Rowen was sleeping in. Carefully, Sonakshi closed her bedroom door and snuck down the hall after Kiera, bare feet silent on the cold stone floor.

"Silver Sparrow has left the nest," whispered Sonakshi, meeting Kiera at the corner where two hallways met. "And I thought you were Red Rosella?"

"I like Willie Wagtail better," Kiera whispered back, peering around the corner. "Can you see anything with your unicorn eyes?"

With her golden eyes, Sonakshi could see better in the dark than anyone she knew.

"Nothing. It's all clear."

"Roger that, Silver Sparrow. Willie Wagtail is headed for the front kitchen corridor. I repeat. Front kitchen corridor. Meet you there." She sprang into the hallway like a deer.

The kitchen was far away, right at the other end of the castle and down on the ground floor. Often, it was quicker for them to split up. They had both been taught to pick locks, so if one of them got caught, at least the other could continue on and finish the mission.

Sonakshi watched Kiera skulk into the darkness and was about to follow when she heard a heavy boot-step. Her heart bounced into her throat and she pressed herself against the wall, listening. The walking boots faded, and she peered down the corridor opposite her, seeing the grey back of the guard's uniform walking away. Sighing in relief, she rounded the corner behind her and followed Kiera. But unicorn hearing was also better than human hearing, so Sonakshi heard what Kiera had not. She stopped halfway down the corridor, at another intersection.

This hallway led to her parents' room, and here, low voices were heatedly arguing. *People* were arguing. She turned into that corridor instead and lurked outside her parents' closed door.

"... it'll be fine," said Father in a soothing voice. Light footsteps were moving up and down the room inside.

"How do we know!" said mother, her voice irritated and anxious. "What if she learns to fly? She is too free-spirited, she won't be able to help it, and someone will see her!"

"She promised she wouldn't. Sampson will keep her in line."

"She's ten, Devin! And Kiera is a bad influence. They run around the castle—"

"It's not Kiera," said her father.

Her mother sighed, "I know. Her unicorn side wants to be free. Unicorns are not made to be caged."

"Let them be children," her father said soothingly, "God knows what will happen when she grows older."

"It's freaking me out knowing *why* we're teaching her to pick locks. Why we're keeping things from her—"

Sonakshi's heart leapt into her throat.

"Come on Ria, you've seen the letter from Fiji. Mankini is on her deathbed. She is not after Sonakshi anymore—"

"She's a witch, Devin! And you know as well as I do what drinking unicorn blood does to a person. Mankini is deformed, not dying."

Sonakshi stepped away from the door in horror.

"I mean, her horn would be so valuable in the wrong hands. Did you see it today?"

"Stop it, Ria. Sampson will protect her—"

Sonakshi had heard enough.

Mankini is deformed…

The vision of a weathered, horrible face swam into her vision. She had seen it in her dreams; it had haunted her sleep since she was three. She ran down the corridor and back to her room, closing the door and pressing herself against it.

That name... *Mankini.*

This witch had drunk unicorn blood?

Whose unicorn blood?

And now she was after her. She had always known that someone had been after her, but she had never managed to put a name to the face she'd seen in her nightmares. She crawled back into bed and lay there, trying not to see the haggard woman...

Minutes later, Sonakshi's bedroom door opened, and Sonakshi jumped. But it was only Kiera, panting, clutching a brown packet in her hand.

"I got it! Where were you?" she asked, bending over, hands on her knees. "I haven't worked that hard since my parents took me skiing in the Swiss Alps."

When Sonakshi didn't reply, Kiera looked up, frowning. "What's wrong? Did they catch you again?"

"No, they didn't. I guess I caught them."

Kiera sat on the bed, placing the chocolate packet to the side. She was worried at the look on Sonakshi's face—haunted, and serious.

"What do you mean?"

Sonakshi wondered how much she should tell her best friend. She looked at Kiera's concerned eyes and knew she could trust her.

"You know how I have those nightmares about that scary lady that's coming to get me?"

"Yeah."

"Well, I just found out her name."

CHAPTER THREE

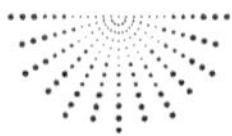

To take the life of a unicorn requires a black heart. He with a sound, red-blooded heart could never conceive, even for a moment, of committing such an atrocity.
To see a unicorn is to feel wonder and awe. To see a unicorn is to know love. To kill a unicorn is to ignore all these things in your natural heart and look the other way. An action that can only be done by a being who actively chooses untruth, who actively chooses the self above all, who actively chooses darkness.
—Lord Anthony Godfrey, *The Annals of Unicorn sightings of the 16th Century, 1701.*

Mankini's Fortress, Makogai Island, Fiji

In an old, withered chair sat an old, withered woman, thinking old, withered thoughts. Mankini Mataitoga was not a regular witch. In her days of youth, she had been powerful, beautiful, and feared. One hundred and fifty years later, however, she was powerless, disfigured, and feared only for a reputation borne of evil deeds long forgotten by the residents of Fiji.

She had slain dragons and cursed kings, but her current sorry state was due to a monumental error in judgement. The burden of immortality was a heavy one. But the burden of slaying a unicorn to gain it was even greater.

To kill a unicorn meant gaining a never-ending life and a never-ending curse.

And so she sat in her great fortress of cold stone, too fearful to leave lest anyone see what her face and body had become. One eye was twice the size of the other, and milky white. Her nose sat twisted on one side of her face, her white lips on the opposite side. Her back was so hunched she could barely walk on her spindly, weak legs, and her fingers were bent with an arthritis so fierce it hurt to hold a cup of water, or a knife.

"Batuman!" she croaked angrily. Patience had never been her strong suit.

The obese bat, thrice as tall as a regular bat from magical exposure in his early years, wobbled over, a tray of tea and Scotch shortbread finger biscuits held high in the air.

"Coming, Mistress!" he cooed, ever patient, ever watchful, and ever loyal. He set the tray by the old table at her side and hoisted himself up with great effort, sitting on her knee.

"How old am I today, Batuman?" she asked, opening her mouth wide. Batuman broke a Scotch finger into quarters with claws attached to spiky winged arms, and placed a piece on her hairy pink tongue.

"One hundred and ninety today, I believe."

"Hmm." She chewed, her jowls moving in a slow rhythmic circle.

"That means…" Her face screwed up in thought. "… That means your attempts to kidnap the unicorn princess have failed for ten years."

She looked at him sternly. "You have been failing me for *ten years.*"

"Yes, Mistress. It is *all* my fault, Mistress."

Batuman bowed as low as he could over his large tummy.

She slammed a bony fist down on the armrest of the chair, sending china clattering in all directions, and Batuman rolled off her lap and landed on the floor with a heavy thud.

"Don't give me lip, boy!"

She sighed and attempted to straighten her shoulders, brushing crumbs from her black dress. "I am old, Batuman, and tired."

Batuman shuffled slowly up to her, eyes glazed with loyal tears.

"Batuman has been taking care of his Mistress well, yes?"

Mankini grumbled something he cannot hear. It did not exactly sound as though she was satisfied with the care she had received.

"I am *old,* Batuman!" she shouted at him, and he

cowered at her feet. "I have been stuck in this chair for a whole week." She slammed the armrest again. "I cannot be stuck for eternity in this chair! I need this curse to be removed, and I want my powers back!"

The room reverberated with her demanding, petulant cries.

Batuman shrank, as if he tried to hide himself within his own skin.

"You hear me, Batuman?"

"I hear, but... How, Mistress?" Batuman cried in a plaintive little voice, tears streaming down his hairy cheeks. "The princess is protected so well, that even with her parents away, kidnap is impossible! There must be another way!"

Mankini took her teacup from the table next to her and hurled it.

It shattered against the wall, in a spray of hot tea and china.

The shards from the fractured cup joined the others on the floor.

"There is no other way!" she shouted. Batuman cowered further into the skirts at her feet.

"You know as well as I do, Batuman," she said gently, while peering down at him, "there is no other way. A curse made by a unicorn can only be corrected by another unicorn. I need her blood. All of it. Nothing less."

She scratched her chin with long, yellowed fingernails.

"We need to rethink this," she murmured to herself. "We need a new strategy."

Batuman took the opportunity to climb up the chair onto the armrest. He sat panting.

"We can't go to her," he mused. "If only we could get her to come to us."

"I have it!" Mankini shouted. "We get her to come to us!"

Batuman nodded reasonably.

"Very good idea, Madam, very good. I would never have thought of that."

"Get me a pen and paper," she commanded. "I need to write a couple of letters."

Batuman looked at the long way he had to climb down.

"You will need to lose weight, Batuman," she said, jabbing a finger into his fat cheek. "Otherwise, you might fall and drown on the way."

"On the way?"

"Oh yes," she smiled. "Because I need *you* to deliver the letters."

"Can we not use a carrier pigeon like we do to send messages to your servants there? I mean..."

His voice jittered. He was thinking, fast.

"I mean, wouldn't it be better for the carrier pigeon to show up and—"

She set one beady eye on him, the larger one looking in another direction.

"Oh, no Batuman. They've screwed this up too many times. No. I will need you to go in person."

Batuman gulped.

"Yes, Madam. Anything for you, Madam."

CHAPTER FOUR

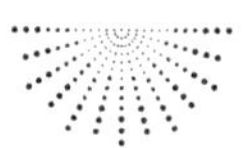

The unicorn knows the natural timings of the world. All things happen in accordance with the grand design. Summer must follow spring. Darkness must follow the night. And evil must follow the good.
—Lord Anthony Godfrey, *The Annals of Unicorn Sightings in the 16th Century, 1701.*

The girls and Rowen awoke early the next morning to say goodbye to their parents, walking bleary-eyed to the main hall. They waved, as the four of them plus two guards left on horses into the bush towards the city harbour, where they would board a large ship for Sydney.

The girls returned to Sonakshi's room to find a large, fat, hairy creature on her bed.

"Aagh!"

They cried out, clinging onto each other. Sonakshi

reached for the door handle and was about to yank it open and call the guard *when the thing* spoke through a strange, tiny mouth.

"It's ok! It's ok! It's just me, Batuman!"

Sonakshi froze, and the girls both turned to stare at the ugly thing that spoke as if it knew them. It spoke in an odd, high-pitched, singsong voice.

"What did you say?" asked Sonakshi, cautiously.

"I *said*, it's just me."

The *thing* made a movement with its face, that almost looked like a smile.

Sonakshi glanced at Kiera who looked at her and shrugged as if to say, *well, I don't know!* She stepped forward to take a better look at it.

It, too, hopped forward on her bed, toward her.

"Yes, yes, come closer," it said.

The thing was very round in face and tummy, and covered in coarse black hair. It had long pointed ears, a little black snout, and leathery wings that ended with tiny claws. It wore a small brown satchel diagonally across its body.

It was, with no mistake, a bat. Just a very large one. Maybe even one that couldn't fly, since surely, its humongous belly would weigh it down?

They didn't know what to make of it.

"I have travelled oh so far to see you, my dear," the bat said gently.

"Really?" she asked, feeling Kiera coming to stand next to her.

It nodded with its eyes closed.

"Very far. The last time I saw you, you were very little. Yes, so tiny."

Sonakshi felt her heart skip a beat. "What? You saw me when I was little?"

"Oh, yes, just a tiny unicorn foal."

Sonakshi and Kiera exchanged a look. No one outside of their property in the Blue Mountains was supposed to know about her being a unicorn.

"When was this?" she asked slowly.

"In Fiji."

Sonakshi's mind raced, but the bat stepped forward and said quickly. "You were just a baby, tiny and innocent, and I just wanted to be your friend."

Sonakshi stepped back.

"Sona, I don't think—" Kiera began.

But the bat thing jumped forward, holding its claws up in submission.

"Oh, no, please! I don't mean any harm, I just have a message to give you."

Sonakshi gulped.

"From whom? I don't usually receive messages."

"From a teacher. A teacher of such great power and knowledge. Here it is."

The bat brought out a tiny piece of folded paper from its satchel.

"Please read it, I have come a long way to give it to you."

Sonakshi took hold of the yellowed, wrinkled paper, which did indeed look as though it had come a long, long way.

. . .

Dear Sonakshi,

Hello, my name is Mona, and I knew you when you were very young. I have come across some very important information that I MUST share with you. Your parents have been keeping vital information from you. Without it, you will never be a true unicorn and NEVER gain your true powers. They fear hidden power and what you can really do.

No one I have met has this information. It can only be passed down from unicorn to unicorn. Please, I believe you are the last one. Let it not die along with me, Sonakshi.

All I require in return is a single drop of your blood.

I am very unwell and close to death. This will save my life.

I will send a ship to pick you up in four days' time from Freshwater Bay.

I implore you, do not let your people down.

Mona

Fiji Islands

Sonakshi stared at the bat, her mind racing. Her parents were keeping information from her…

Well, that part she knew to be true already, from listening to them the other night. But was it really because they were fearful of her? She knew she was different, but did that mean they were scared of her? But the last part made everything irrelevant.

I will send a ship for you.

"I cannot leave here sir. My parents—"

"They want to hide things from you. Keep you in the dark. Keep you away from your powers. These are things they do not understand. How could they? You're the only one."

Sonakshi frowned, scratching the back of her head. Batuman was saying things she had already been thinking on her own. Her parents certainly did not want her to fly and wanted to keep her hidden. But the hidden part was for very good reason, wasn't it?

This supposed Mona came from Fiji, where she was born.

The witch, Mankini, also came from there. Was it a coincidence? Hmm…

"I don't know about Mankini's letter…" she said.

"I will give you some time to think about it," Batuman said, reasonably.

"Ha!"

He jumped.

"So it is Mankini, not Mona!" she narrowed her eyes at the bat.

But Batuman shrugged it off.

"Mona is a nickname, Princess. Just a nickname."

It was all too much. The tricks, the lying, her parents and now this vile creature. Her heart pounded in her ears. She had caught the bat thing out; it had come here to try and deceive and trick her, acting on behalf of Mankini. Mona… Mankini… one and the same.

"I don't believe anything you say!" Sonakshi blurted out. "They are my parents. They want what is best for me. You're trying to trick me."

Batuman placed a claw over his heart, and his eyes went wide. "Me? Batuman? Never!"

He flew haphazardly from the bed to the windowsill.

"I, Batuman, am always kind and generous—I flew over the Pacific Ocean for you!"

"Well, you've wasted your time, I'm afraid. I can't do any of the things you ask."

Batuman paused at the sill, then turned and said in a strange tone, "Have any of your powers come in yet?" Sonakshi did not like the way the thing's voice made goosebumps ripple all over her skin. Powers? Which powers was she supposed to have? She wanted to know more!

"That's none of your business!" said Kiera from the side, crossing her arms.

Batuman made a small silent "ah" with his mouth, and nodded.

"Of course not. How *could* your powers come in? You do not have the right teachers here."

"I am not interested," said Sonakshi, frowning deeply at him. And it was true, of course. She wasn't interested, was she?

"Then," Batuman said slowly and mercilessly, "You will never be a *real* unicorn."

Batuman's words hit Sonakshi in the heart like an arrow.

CHAPTER FIVE

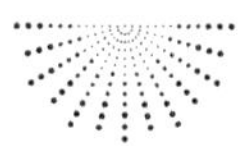

There are moments in our lives that change the course of our destiny. In these moments lies a decision, an action or inaction. Hence, it is by your decisions that you carve out your destiny from the brilliant cave that is life.
—Lord Anthony Godfrey, *his personal diary, 1688*

The next morning, everything changed.

The girls awoke to frantic yelling. They jumped out of bed, running out of Sonakshi's bedroom and into the corridor, dressing gowns flying.

"Oh Kiera!" Tammy ran down the corridor, blonde hair a mess, and flung her arms around Kiera and Sonakshi both. "Oh Sona!"

"What's happened?" asked Sonakshi.

Tammy wiped tears down her lined face and blubbered, "They've taken Rowen! He's gone in the middle of the night, I didn't notice, how could I not have noticed?"

She sobbed into a handkerchief.

Kiera pushed past her and ran into the room Rowen had used when he was there, Sonakshi close behind. Three guards searched the room. It was true; the bed was empty with the covers thrown back, and the curtains—the curtains were billowing in the wind from the open window.

"You two!"

Captain Sampson came up from behind them as they stared open-mouthed at the scene.

"I need you two to stay in Princess Sonakshi's room."

"Where is Rowen?" asked Kiera in a small voice.

Sampson bent down on one knee and placed a gentle hand on her shoulder. "I will get him back, Kiera, I promise."

It was Kiera's turn to cry. "Where is he?"

Sonakshi gathered Kiera in her arms, and Sampson sighed.

"Someone we have known for a very long time. Someone we have been protecting both you girls from has finally gotten in. Mankini, a witch from the Pacific has taken him."

"Why would she take *him*?" asked Sonakshi in shock.

Sampson stared at the open bedroom window and hesitated. "I—"

Sonakshi had a bad, bad feeling. The witch from Fiji was supposed to be after *her*. "Tell me, Sampson."

Sampson did not meet her eye when he spoke.

"The letter she left leads me to believe she mistakenly took him instead of you."

Sonakshi's heart sank and Kiera stopped crying to stare at him.

"But that's stupid! Everybody knows that Sona is a *girl*," Kiera said, wiping her nose with the back of her sleeve.

"Yes. However, I believe Mankini sent others to do her kidnap. And they made the mistake."

"I want to see the note," demanded Kiera.

"It's—very distressing. I don't think you should see it."

"I don't care!"

"Tammy, take the girls to their room please."

"I don't want to go—" Kiera began.

"Kiera, I will get him back. She has indicated where they are taking him. I *will* get him back. I promise you that."

Tammy appeared in the corridor and Sampson strode out the door. Kiera tried to follow, but Tammy blocked her. "Kiera, we need to make sure there is not a repeat attempt." She steered Kiera by the shoulders, combing her messy red hair with her fingers, speaking in gentle tones.

Sonakshi's heart hung somewhere near her knees.

It was supposed to be *her* that was taken. She couldn't believe that poor Rowen had gotten caught up in this. He was only a tiny boy five years. What were they going to do with him?

That bat! It was responsible. It was *all* the bat's

doing! She couldn't believe he had spoken to her as a friend.

Sonakshi's suspicions were confirmed just an hour later. They were alone in her room, with a guard stationed outside her door and beneath her second-story window. They had watched Sampson lead most of the guard out the front gates, astride horses, galloping into the bushland. Sitting on the floor, holding Kiera in her arms, they heard a light *tap tap* on the window. They both jumped up and stared at the curtains. Sonakshi could see a large round shadow sitting there.

"Batuman," she hissed, rushing to the window, preparing to throw the bat down to the ground. She parted the curtain and saw the thing sitting there, an unfriendly smile on its face.

No longer did it looks like the same smarmy grinning thing trying to win her over.

She unlatched the window.

"Good morning," Batuman said in a singsong voice.

"You!" Kiera said, pointing at the bat. "*You* did this!"

He held his claws up and flew over to the bed.

Sonakshi vaguely wondered, for the second time, how that over-stuffed creature managed to fly at all.

"I tried to be polite, Your Highness," he bowed, mockingly. "But you have been very rude and refused my most generous offer."

Sonakshi did not know what to say. This was all her fault.

"So I had to give you an offer you could not refuse."

"And what's that?"

"Present yourself to Makogai Island to give a single drop of your blood and we will return little Rowen unharmed. Do not give your blood, and we will drop Rowen into a shark-infested lagoon. Simple. See? My mistress just wants to live. That's all we need, just one drop."

Sonakshi turned to Kiera, but her friend's attention remained on Batuman.

"You horrible little—"

Sonakshi grabbed Kiera around the waist just in time, and Batuman flew back over to the windowsill.

"They're going after him anyway," said Sonakshi calmly. "My guards are getting Rowen back. He won't even get as far as Fiji."

"Ahhhhhh," said Batuman, shaking his head wildly. "See, I already thought of that. We have led your guards somewhere else."

He began laughing in a choking evil way, and the girls cringed. "They have gone in completely the wrong direction. I needed a way to get you a clear path out of this castle."

Kiera stopped fighting Sonakshi's grip and went limp.

"So… you see," Batuman said, "the only way you get your little boy back, is if you come and get him yourself. And if you tell anyone, I promise you I will feed him to the sharks anyway." He went to jump out of the window. "A ship arrives for you at Freshwater Bay in four days," he added, beginning to extend his wings. "Goodbye."

He was gone.

Sonakshi and Kiera sank down to the floor.

"What is happening!"

"I don't know!" moaned Kiera.

"This is crazy. Absolutely nuts. We should tell Tammy."

"No!" Kiera cried, then glanced the door and hastily lowered her voice. "You heard him, they'll kill him anyway. They just want your blood! They don't even care about Rowen!"

"Don't say that!" said Sonakshi, "Don't—"

"But it's true! He said that all they want is a drop of your blood, remember?"

Sonakshi sat silently. "What can I do, Kiera? I'm not allowed to leave."

Kiera cast her eye out the window. "More than half of the guard is gone, it wouldn't be that hard—"

"Kiera! I'm forbidden to leave here, I just can't—"

"Don't you want Rowen back?" Kiera stared at her, lips pressed tightly together.

"Yes! But I just can't leave here. There has to be another way."

"Well, there isn't." She stood. "I thought you were my friend."

Kiera's face crumpled, and tears streamed down her cheeks.

"Please, Sona, you're supposed to be my friend!"

Sonakshi jumped up. "I am! I *am* your friend, Kiera! But it's impossible—"

"It's not! Sona, please. Just give them what they want. It's not much."

"I mean—it is. We'd have to travel through the

bushland and sail over the ocean. How are *we* supposed to do that?"

"I've gone there heaps of times." Kiera shrugged. "It's easy, just a straight path through the bush."

Sonakshi sighed. She felt as if she was going to throw up. Her heart pounded in her chest. "I can't, Kiera. It's not going to—"

Kiera turned on her foot and pounded her hand against the door three times, and the door vibrated in its frame. Guard Laurie opened the door, peering in, suspiciously.

"I want to be in a separate room!" Kiera cried.

He peered at them both and then, seeing the tears on both their faces he nodded, beckoning Kiera to come outside the room, and she strode out into the corridor without looking back.

CHAPTER SIX

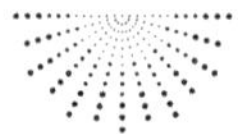

Three things come naturally to the Unicorn. Love, Resilience and Sacrifice.
—Lord Anthony Godfrey, *The Annals of Unicorn Sightings of the 16th Century, 1701.*

Sonakshi curled up on the floor in her room, alone. Her chest felt like lead and her tummy churned, feeling as though it was going to throw up her breakfast at any second.

How had everything gone wrong so quickly?

One second, and all three of them had been happy and laughing, and were safe—and the next, it was all gone. Rowen had been taken instead of her, and Kiera was furious

She had never left the palace grounds. *Ever.*

She needed to talk to someone. She needed advice.

She walked over to her desk and brushed her fingers along the cover of the beautiful bound book of unicorn paintings her father had given her last Christmas. They looked so powerful and strong. Why didn't she feel like that?

What was the difference between her and all the unicorns in those pictures?

Batuman's words haunted her mind and spirit, weighing her down as if a pile of wood was sitting on her shoulders. *You will never be a real unicorn.*

It must be true. She was not a real unicorn.

She was a fake and a fraud. People laughed at her, not gazing at her with awe and wonder like the other unicorns. All they ever did was tell her off.

"I asked my great-grandmother about my great-grandfather once," her own mother had told her one night, brushing out her long black hair in lengthy, sweeping motions. "And she said that he was so beautiful that to see him was to weep."

"But he loved her," Sonakshi had said in wonder. "She must have been a very special lady."

Sonakshi's mother had smiled at her, saying, "Sometimes, I wonder... how could a unicorn fall in love with a human?"

"But *I* love you."

Her mother had laughed and wiped her eyes, pulling Sonakshi into a warm embrace.

"And I love you, my little unicorn."

If only Sonakshi could *speak* to another unicorn, to learn and understand what it was all about. She wasn't even sure of the powers she had. And if there really were all these people after her, how could she possibly defend herself?

Why did she have to be the only one around?

She had a lot of questions and the people who could answer them were rare.

Rowen's chubby face swam in her mind's eye. Her eyes burned and more tears streamed down her face. They had taken Rowen in *her* place. It should have been her being kidnapped and taken away, not a poor, helpless, red-headed and stupid boy.

Can you just go somewhere else? Can you just go away?

She couldn't believe she had said all these things to him, and they had come true.

Whichever way she looked at it, this was all her fault.

She had to fix this, or she'd never forgive herself—and worse, Kiera would never forgive her either. She saw her path in her mind's eye. This was the only way. To do exactly what Mankini said. Just a single drop of her blood, and Rowen would be set free.

And they couldn't tell anyone.

It honestly didn't sound too hard, did it? And Kiera had travelled heaps; she would know her way through to Freshwater Bay for sure.

She stood. And opened her door. Laurie looked at her in surprise.

"I need to talk to Kiera."

He nodded and escorted her to the room Rowen had been sleeping in. Guard Alex was standing in front of it. Sonakshi gulped and knocked.

After a few tense moments, Kiera opened it a crack, one green eye peering out.

Sonakshi pushed open the door and closed it quickly behind her.

“Listen Sona,” began Kiera, rubbing her neck awkwardly. “I’m sorry I said…”

“Let’s do this.”

Kiera’s mouth dropped open.

“What? You mean—?”

Sonakshi nodded. “We’re going to listen to Batuman. I think he was being honest when he said he would hurt Rowen if we don’t.”

Kiera nodded seriously. “I think so too.”

“We sneak out all the time. We can do it again.”

“I overheard the guards talking,” Kiera said, not meeting Sonakshi’s eye. “They’re not telling our parents about this. They’re frightened.”

Sonakshi blew out air from her cheeks.

“They might change their minds about that when we’ve gone too. But it gives us a head start, at least. And that’s got to be good for us.”

Kiera stuck out her hand and looked at her with serious, glistening eyes.

A single tear trailed down her cheek.

“Sona, you know you’ll always be my best friend. I knew you wanted to help Rowen.”

Sonakshi rushed forward and threw her arms around Kiera.

“I could have not wished for a better best friend. And I’m so, so sorry Rowen got taken instead of me. It should have been me…”

She sobbed, amazed that Kiera could even look her in the eye after all this.

Kiera just hugged her harder.

CHAPTER SEVEN

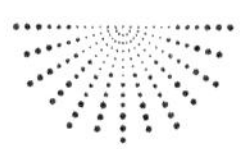

He heard the scuffle of the animals in the forest around him. He heard the beating of my fluttering heart. And I was almost certain that his hearing was so advanced he could hear my very soul.
—Lord Anthony Godfrey, *The Annals of Unicorn Sightings of the 16th century, 1701.*

"Backpack?"

"Check."

"Tent and sleeping bag?"

"Check and check."

"Food?"

"Um—check."

Sonakshi ticked her list and took a deep breath. It was an hour before dawn, and now was their best chance to leave without being stopped. Tammy was still snoring next door and Kiera was shoving more food from the stash under the bed into a bag.

"Then I believe we are ready."

Sonakshi placed a letter on her desk for Tammy to find. She had written that they were going after Captain Sampson and the group to help them. Hopefully, that would keep the remaining guards from finding out where they were really heading. If they could get a solid head start to Freshwater Bay, they would be off to Fiji in no time at all.

She peered out her window. Guard Andrew was standing directly below it; she knew it by his sandy coloured hair and long nose. And at barely sixteen, he might just fall for a diversion.

"Psst! Andrew!" Sonakshi hissed.

He looked up, startled.

"I saw something over there!"

"Where?"

"Over there in the scrub!"

She pointed into the distant bush, in the opposite direction of the path they had to take.

Immediately, he ran off towards where she was pointing, holding his spear high.

"Quick!" hissed Sonakshi, and Kiera brought over the twisted bed sheets they had knotted together and tied to her sturdy bed. Sonakshi went first. Dropping her backpack on to the ground, she climbed out of the windowsill and—gripping onto the sheet so that her knuckles turned white—she balanced her feet against the stone wall.

Awkwardly, she relaxed her grip reluctantly, her

heart pounding in her chest as if it was trying to break free of her ribcage. Little by little, just an inch at a time, she began to let herself down, walking her feet down the stone. Once she landed on the soft grass, Kiera did the same.

Sonakshi checked behind her, but thankfully, Andrew was still off into the forest and the dark grounds were silent and empty.

Once Kiera had reached the ground too, it only took a few attempts to swing the bed sheet back up into Sonakshi's room. They bolted through the night, into the dark mountain pass.

Lucky for Sonakshi, Kiera took this path all the time because it was the way to her home in Cabbage Tree Creek. She knew every centimetre of this route, every stone, every leaf.

It was a serious uphill walk for some time, however, and Sonakshi was seriously out of breath. She huffed and puffed, and their breaths made foggy clouds in the cold pre-dawn air.

"We should've gotten horses," panted Kiera, wiping sweat off her forehead.

"We'd definitely get caught that way," Sonakshi said.

There was no way they could have stolen some horses without being seen.

Eventually, they reached the top of the pass and stared down at the bush before them. The sky had lightened with that strange blue-grey colour that always came before the dawn.

As far as the eye could see, vibrant green bushland lay before them, a never-ending sea of green between them and Freshwater Bay. Batuman had said a ship would wait for them in four days. Would it be enough time to trek through this forest? *Four days,* Sonakshi thought, *is a long time to be travelling alone.* And she was already feeling quite worn out.

Her father had taken her for walks around the mountain path, but she had never gone any farther, let alone without him. It looked like the eucalyptus and the gum trees would be their only friends on this mission, as long as they didn't meet anyone or anything else. And, of course, she hoped very much that of they did encounter something, it wouldn't be as horrible and creepy as Batuman. She thought back to her first sight of the thing, shuddering.

Kiera took a long drink of water while Sonakshi stared lamely at the path ahead.

Her heart pounded in her ears again, and the cold air bit at her throat.

This was it. They were really doing this, and they were really, entirely, alone.

All the things that could go wrong ran through her brain like a hamster on a wheel. The trip to Freshwater Bay was dangerous, let alone the actual rescuing part.

Was she crazy?

Was Kiera crazy?

Did they really want to get themselves killed, or at least horribly disoriented and lost in the bush? Strangers on the road, wandering off their supposed route, not finding water. These were the awful things people talked about all the time, and about how bones would turn up in the forest, in caves, on exposed hilltops... bones of adventurers who also hadn't had a clue.

What else did she not know? Her teachers had taught her so much about the world, but seeing it with her own golden eyes was a different matter entirely.

A long and arduous journey loomed ahead of them. Were they ready? Kiera might be, having travelled with her family so much. She might not find this too difficult. But Sonakshi herself, having never stepped foot outside of her home, was she even slightly ready for the world? And if she couldn't control herself and turned into a unicorn?

What would real, outside people think if they saw something such as that, a strange beast? She imagined being locked in a cell far away from home with strangers gaping at her. And she imagined taking an arrow through her heart, just so someone greedy could saw off her diamond horn and get rich from it. Sure, somebody could make a lot of money showing a unicorn at a circus, but they would get even more—and in one fell swoop—if they simply sold her horn.

Then her mother's voice came into her ear.

I'm freaking out, thinking about why we taught her to pick locks.

Sonakshi shivered, right to her bones.

Next to her, Kiera deeply inhaled the fresh morning air.

"We're coming, Rowen," she whispered to herself. "You get ready for us!"

Sonakshi heard this, and any fear or guilt she had

for leaving against her parents' wishes disappeared immediately. This was the only way to rescue Rowen.

It just had to be done, no ifs or buts, no excuses.

Rowen would *not* die because she was too fearful and weak to travel to him.

Steeling herself, Sonakshi resolutely began the downward walk, Kiera close behind.

The rocky ground eventually gave way to softer, dark soil, and the trees grew dense around them. Kiera said that if they followed the path straight through the bush, and turned when the signs said so, they would be back on track easily. It would be hard to get lost, she said.

Content with this, Sonakshi stared wide-eyed at the surrounding bushland, enjoying the smell of the different trees. She smelled eucalyptus, bottlebrush, and gum trees. The birds laughed and chirped about her and far into the distance. Animals scurried and rustled in the bushes, and at one stage, she even thought she heard the gruff snuffling of an echidna.

They walked for some time through the bush, and as the sky became bright blue, Sonakshi noted something different about the sounds her keen ears were picking up.

Rustle shuffle, rustle shuffle, rustle.

It was so quiet she might have missed it if she were not concentrating. Kiera's human ears definitely would not have been able to pick it up. Sonakshi listened with determination.

It was consistent and did not fade away like the

other sounds. As they walked, the rustling stayed the same. When they stopped to sip water, it too, halted.

When they started walking again, it restarted.

An icy trickle of fear ran down her chest.

“Kiera,” Sonakshi whispered, staring straight ahead.

“Yeah?”

“Don’t stop walking, but I think we’re being followed.”

CHAPTER EIGHT

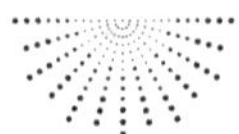

I have seen a unicorn horn in all its glory, solid glittering diamond with powers mostly unknown. I have seen a unicorn deliver a mortal wound to an animal with that horn. I have seen it give revival at the moment of death to the very same animal. Touch it with your bare skin and it will cut you. It is as sharper than the sharpest knife known to man. A wound made by a unicorn speaks a different language than other wounds.

— Lord Andrew Godfrey, *The Annals of Unicorn Sightings of the 16th Century, 1701.*

Kiera faltered in her step, but kept walking, her eyes wide. Sonakshi could tell she was itching to look back and see what it was. "What do we do?" Sonakshi whispered.

Sonakshi had been hoping Kiera would know the answer.

Had she not been followed before in any of her travels?

No, she decided. This was an unusual and unfortunate thing.

Had someone from home followed them? No, that couldn't be it. They would have made themselves known and marched them straight back to the Valley. The strangest thing was that the sound their follower was making wasn't one she'd expect from a person wearing shoes or boots. There was more *air* to it, less crunch. Whatever it was had an elongated stride.

An icicle of fear shot through her again.

"Kiera … you don't know of any large animals out here, do you?" she whispered. "Animals that prey on humans?"

Kiera turned her head slowly to look at her, green eyes bulging. Her whisper held a note of panic. "Why would you ask that?"

"Because… Whatever is following us isn't a human."

Kiera's face screwed up, and she pulled at her collar. "Oh no. How big is it?"

"It's hard to tell. But we need to sort this out."

"Sort it out?" she whispered hysterically. "How do you propose we *sort it out*?"

Sonakshi stopped abruptly in her tracks and turned, squaring her shoulders. Their follower stopped too. Kiera almost fell over. She surveyed the path now in front of her. It was empty.

But she looked at the bushland on their left and noticed a slight movement behind a dense green bush. "I see you!" she called, pointing a finger at the bush.

Kiera tore at her hair, then grabbed at Sonakshi's arm, panicked.

"What are you doing?" Sonakshi hissed. "Come out, sir!" Sonakshi then called, fearlessly, confronting.

She wondered why she had decided it was a sir.

But it was too late now, so she just went with it.

"Hello?" Sonakshi cried, loudly and without a tremor in her tone. "Look. If you don't show yourself, I'm going to come right in there after you!"

Shoot! She hadn't thought of what she was going to say before that sort of slipped out.

Was she actually going to stomp into the bush after an unknown stalker?

Kiera, inspired by Sonakshi's sudden bravery, bent down and grabbed something from the ground. Before Sonakshi could stop her, she hurled a large rock into the bush where Sonakshi had pointed. There was a small thump and a thud, and suddenly, a greyish-brown head fell into view at the bottom of the bush. "Ow!" came a high-pitched voice.

Sonakshi could not help it; the sudden voice, mixed with her suppressed fear and adrenaline, made her explode into her unicorn form.

"Sona!" cried Kiera in dismay.

But Sonakshi's heart pounded, and she remained transfixed by the bush.

Whatever she'd been expecting, it was not a female human-like voice.

But when the figure hobbled out from behind the bush, looking somewhat dazed, it wasn't human at all.

It was brown-haired with oval ears standing up straight, and a dark snout.

The kangaroo gasped and pointed at Sonakshi. "Oh, then it's true!"

Kiera groaned with a mixture of surprise and dismay. But Sonakshi was too busy staring at the kangaroo in front of them, to register what it was saying. *Saying...?*

"Did you just speak?" she asked in shock.

The kangaroo opened its mouth, then closed it and suddenly covered its mouth with a paw.

"Did you hear it speak?" she turned to Kiera. "Or did I just imagine that?"

Kiera's face had turned the colour of a strawberry and all she could do was nod.

Sonakshi, still in her unicorn form, walked a few steps closer to the kangaroo that watched her with shocked black eyes.

"Can you really speak?" she asked more gently. "I mean… you speak English?"

The kangaroo nodded and uncovered her mouth. "Are you really a unicorn?"

Sonakshi inwardly chastised herself and hastily changed back into her girl form.

"Yes, I am."

"Then you're the unicorn princess."

Sonakshi exhaled and turned to glance at Kiera, who gave her a sympathetic look. Sonakshi shrugged at the kangaroo. They saw kangaroos all the time around the valley.

Clearly, these creatures spoke to one another somehow.

"Why were you following us?" Sonakshi asked.

The kangaroo scratched her chest.

"I—well, you see… I just saw you walking down the path and wanted to get a better look at you."

"At me?" asked Sonakshi.

She nodded.

"Why can you talk?"

"Plenty of the animals here can talk. If you're around fae when you are a child, it happens."

"Fae?"

"Hey! Where's your tail?" Kiera said in horror.

Sonakshi stared. She should've seen it sooner, but she had been distracted.

Indeed, the kangaroo was without a tail. In its place was the tiniest of stumps.

"I was attacked by a bat," she replied self-consciously. "I have it here—"

She bent down and picked up a hemp bag from behind her.

"You kept your tail in your bag?" asked Kiera, wrinkling her nose.

"Well, I couldn't just leave it." She slung her bag over her shoulder. "I'm attached to it."

Kiera's and Sonakshi's eyebrows rose. They didn't want to state the obvious.

But anyway, Sonakshi was more concerned about what had attacked her.

"What type of bat?" she asked, glancing at Kiera to see if she got her meaning.

"Oh, just a regular bat… it had sharp claws. But anyway. I need to find a fae doctor to fix it. I'm hoping they can put it back on. I feel kind of unbalanced… especially when I jump."

"A fae doctor?" asked Sonakshi.

"Yes, they are the only type of people that can help me. They're just really hard to find."

Sonakshi and Kiera exchanged an uncertain look. Fae? Really? All of this was very unexpected.

"What are they exactly?" asked Kiera, curiously stepping forward.

"Oh, you know—" the kangaroo waved her arms in a wide arc. "They have these large wings and multi-coloured hair."

From a distant memory, the vision of a man with a blue beard swam into Sonakshi's brain. He had helped her parents when they'd left Fiji. She remembered him smiling at her and recalled that he had seemed kind. She also knew he had said something important to her at the time, but she was far better with remembering faces than words.

She suddenly recalled the whole reason they were standing there.

She would have preferred to ask her more questions, but there really wasn't time.

"Look, well it was nice to meet you and all, but we should really get going."

"And it might be better if you didn't mention seeing us to anyone," piped Kiera.

Sonakshi looked at her in surprise.

"Why?" came the kangaroo's, slow, curious voice.

Sonakshi almost groaned.

If the kangaroo hadn't been curious about her before, she was now!

"It's just," explained Sonakshi. "There are people who might want to hurt me."

"You're very honest," said the kangaroo apprais-ingly. "I can't but help wonder where you two are going?"

Kiera grabbed Sonakshi's arm and pulled her away.

"It was nice meeting you," Kiera called over her shoulder, "See you!"

"Well, if you go down that path, you're headed straight into a crocodiles' nest!"

The girls stopped in their tracks.

The kangaroo sighed and bounded forward twice. "And if you're headed to the coast, you're going the wrong way. You should have turned right at the previous fork."

Kiera stomped her foot.

"I knew it!" she groaned. "I thought we should have reached the large wattle tree by now!"

Sonakshi looked at her friend, dumbfounded.

"You weren't even sure where you were going? I thought—"

Kiera gave her an apologetic look. "I kind of do know, but I think it was about the time you said someone was following us that I missed it. I got distracted."

Sonakshi rolled her eyes.

"Well, thanks for telling us—er, I don't know your name, sorry… do you have a name?"

The kangaroo bounded over to them eagerly and held out a paw. “I do! I am Allira.”

Sonakshi shook Allira’s paw and got to look at her up close. She was quite beautiful for a kangaroo, she thought, with incredibly long eyelashes, high cheek-bones, and wide, expressive brown eyes. Sonakshi could feel something when she shook her paw. There seemed to be a grief, a sadness, and a feeling of help-lessness. Sonakshi looked again at the tatty-looking hemp bag she carried in her other hand as Kiera shook Allira’s paw. She supposed a Kangaroo’s tail was pretty important. Allira sort of hopped awkwardly, looking off balance, just as she had said to them. Losing it must be quite the burden. Now, she felt sorry for the poor thing.

“How will you find a fae doctor?” she asked.

“Oh, there are ways… telltale signs. I’ll just know when I see it.”

“See what?”

“The portal into the fae realm, of course.”

Sonakshi bit back a laugh, but then realised Allira was serious. She could see Kiera giving her crazy eyes from behind Allira’s back, but she ignored her.

Well, unicorns were real, so why couldn’t fairies be real too?

Her parents had thought so, after all, they just never really talked about it.

“I can take you the right way,” said Allira, gesturing back the way they had come. “To get you back on the right path.”

“That’s very kind of you,” said Sonakshi.

They followed her down the track for a moment before she could not help herself.

"Have you seen a fae before?"

"Not since I was a child," said Allira sadly. "It's been my life's mission to find them again, but they are almost impossible to find. And now, my very life depends on it. If I cannot get my tail back on, that will be it for me. My balance is all off, I can't travel nearly as fast. I'll be the joke of the family. And I need to travel fast to even survive... with predators around."

And then, in a matter of seconds, their whole situation changed.

A loud crack sounded in the air, so close to her that Sonakshi reflexively turned into her unicorn self. She had been so close to Allira at the time, that when she elongated in size into her unicorn body, Allira stumbled forward, her bag going flying through the air.

Sonakshi lost her balance too, and tumbled on top of Allira.

Kiera screamed piercingly as Sonakshi's sharper-than-knives diamond horn pierced Allira right on the bottom, not far from the already damaged stump.

Sonakshi yelped and got to her hooves.

"Oh my God, Allira, I'm so sorry!"

But Allira would not answer. She remained face first in the dirt. Sonakshi changed back into her human form and was about to leap forward and see if she was okay when Allira started to glow. From the nub where her tail had been removed—grew a completely new tail.

Becoming long and strong, it turned the same

colour as the rest of Allira's brown fur. The light faded, and Sonakshi and Kiera stared at the new tail in shock. Allira got up with a pained groan. Then she jumped into the air as if she'd been shocked by lightning or had realized she was being followed by a giant snake. Looking behind her, she saw her tail and screamed.

"My tail!"

Sonakshi did not know what to say.

"My tail!"

How *had* her tail just appeared like that?

"My tail!"

Allira ran over to Sonakshi and flung her arms around her.

"Thank you! Thank you! Thank you!"

"But I didn't—"

"Sona," interrupted Kiera, looking at her with bulging green eyes. "I think we just found out a new power of yours."

Sonakshi had seen it for herself. The very same light that came from her when she turned—a bright gold—had shone from Allira the moment she'd removed her horn. And then the tail had grown, just like that! She had never seen her horn do anything like it. She had cut apart an apple for Kiera once, and it was a good light in the dark, but that was about it. They had never tried doing anything else with the sharp thing. There was no doubt about it. *She* had done this, or her horn had anyway. A new sense of hope filled her. What other powers would she find she had? She felt giddy with excitement, her hands trembling.

Allira released her, tears streaming down her face, leaving dark tracks on her fur.

"I don't know how to thank you! I owe you a life debt now."

"Oh no," said Sonakshi, grinning, "I think I should be thanking you!"

"Why did you get scared suddenly? Why did you turn?" asked Kiera to Sonakshi.

"I heard a noise, like a loud clap."

"I heard it too," said Allira. "A crocodile trap. But very far away, up the big river north."

"My unicorn ears hear things much more sharply," Sonakshi explained. "It sounded like it was really close to me."

"Well, I guess I should be thanking the poor crocodile, then! It saved my life. You saved me! How do I repay you?" She held her end of her tail in her paw, lovingly examining it. In the other paw, she held the old tail, now no longer needed. She threw the hemp bag into the bush.

"Well…" said Kiera slowly, turning slightly pink. "I don't suppose you could lead us to Freshwater Bay…? I honestly did think I knew the way there, but usually, we turn off soon to go to Cabbage Tree Creek. And after we pass that fork, I'm going to be lost."

Allira nodded vigorously and said that she was most definitely able to show them the way. She knew this bushland like the back of her hand. But first, Allira hopped to the bush where she had cast the old tail stump in its tattered bag, retrieved it, and buried it under a gum tree.

She looked pensive and respectful, as if saying goodbye to the tail at some deep, spiritual level. The girls solemnly watched on, looking down and also paying their final respects.

After that, the three of them shouldered their bags once again and travelled down the path late into the afternoon, laughing after the adrenaline of the whole incident. Allira bounded about, showing off her new and excellent balance, and her new tail that was at least twice as strong and flexible as her old one. So, it seemed the ugly bat had done her an enormous favour.

Sonakshi looked on, happy to see Allira doing so well again. "Look! She's radiant," Sonakshi said quietly to Kiera. "See how she's jumping around all over the place!"

But no reply came. Kiera was too engrossed in thoughts of her own. "Mmm, hmm," she said, eventually. In fact, Kiera was wondering what other things the magical Sonakshi could heal with her horn. She was excited. Now, the world seemed a better place all of a sudden.

Once the sun had set, and the cicadas started to play their loud music while other bush creatures began to settle down for the night, Allira showed them to a safe spot to set up camp, where she thought the spiders and snakes were least likely to get to them.

The girls rolled out their sleeping bags in the small clearing and ate a dinner of sandwiches.

Sonakshi zipped herself up into her sleeping bag and looked up at the night sky, bright with a universe of stars. *I wonder if my parents are looking at the same stars,* she thought meekly. *And I wonder if Tammy wrote to our parents when she found my letter?*

But even if Tammy had sent someone after them both to chase them down, it would take them a whole day or two to realise the girls weren't following the same trail as Sampson at all.

It might take her parents two to three days to find out and return to the Valley. She could sleep easily, knowing that she and Kiera were well on their way to rescuing Rowen.

A fox snuffled in the distance, and she was suddenly very happy about Allira's company. Being out here all alone was the most difficult thing she had ever done.

But somehow, it felt good as well. Finally, she was out of the castle and into the world, standing on her own two feet! But it wasn't going to be all sunshine out here, she knew.

Even the sounds of the animals in the bush were overwhelming and real. A snake could make its way to them in their sleep, or even a tree branch could fall on them. She could hear that Kiera had fallen asleep already, and even Allira's breathing was slow and settled in sleep. She sighed, trying to reassure herself that nothing would happen out in the wild, and that not everyone out here was bad. She had to remind herself that Allira had actually helped them.

Sonakshi wondered whether her father would believe it! But Allira was one of the few, she was sure. Not everyone out here was bound to be as helpful as she was. Not at all.

And there was also the fact that she now knew she

couldn't even trust Kiera's judgement, she had sworn she knew this place inside and out.

In fact, Kiera had been about to lead them right into a crocodile nest!

Anxiously listening to all the sounds of the nightlife crackling and rustling in the bush, interspersed with the occasional loud howl or hoot, it was not until well into the night when exhaustion took her. Finally, Sonakshi fell into a dreamless, reluctant sleep.

CHAPTER NINE

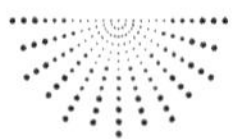

Other animals, if they do not know a unicorn on sight, they will know her for the way she feels. They might not understand it. But they will know.
—Lord Andrew Godfrey, *The Annals of Unicorn Sightings of the 16th Century, 1701.*

Sonakshi and Kiera awoke to kookaburras making a wonderful chorus in the trees nearby. The sky was orange with the dawn light, and the world around them was slowly waking.

"Good morning," said Sonakshi to Allira, who was already up, scratching something down on a piece of paper. She looked up, smiling as best a kangaroo could. But she looked nervous.

"Morning," said Allira, hastily packing her materials back into her bag.

"What are you writing? I probably should also ask

who taught you to write?" Sonakshi asked, rolling up her sleeping bag. "I don't think most kangaroos can even hold a pen?"

"Oh," said Allira, embarrassed, possibly recognizing that her species was not generally filled with literary geniuses. "Well my mother taught me of course. She is quite educated."

Sonakshi smiled at her in surprise. Umm… Kangaroo… *educated?* Really?

"Yes… so I was just writing to her, to tell her all about how my tail came back because of the unicorn! And to tell her about how this tail is better than the last one!"

Sonakshi's smile disappeared. "Umm, Allira," she said, hesitantly, not wanting to offend her new friend. "I'd rather, if it's okay, that you wouldn't mention me to anybody else."

Allira's paws went to her chest. "I'm so sorry, I didn't even think—"

"No, no, it's okay, I just haven't come into this situation before. It's just… no one is supposed to know about me."

Allira scratched her chin. "Except you are travelling in a forest where all the animals will know instantly what you are. They will talk and word will spread. You didn't think the animals would instantly know what you are?"

Sonakshi cringed. She hadn't thought of that. She looked behind her for Kiera's opinion and found her rummaging in their food bag, a pastry stuffed in her mouth.

"Do you really think word will spread that way?" she asked worriedly.

Allira shouldered her hemp bag. "If you are travelling a long way, then yes. Where did you say you were going exactly?"

Sonakshi wondered how much she should tell their new friend. She remembered Allira's face when her tail had reappeared. And she had said she owed her a life debt. Surely that meant they could trust her? But on the other hand, people often said such things and didn't really mean it, just as Dame Marie used to say things like *you'll be the death of me Sona!*

Sonakshi mulled it over. A kangaroo was probably not as fickle as a human. Hmm.

"Come on, Kiera," Sonakshi said. "I think we have to tell Allira our story."

They set back onto the bush trail, rugged up in blankets against the morning chill, munching on pastries while they shared their mission with Allira. The kangaroo listened silently.

"Wow," she said. "I can't believe they took your brother!"

"Yeah," said Kiera, "They're awful people."

They walked the rest of the morning and into the afternoon at a good pace. As the air heated, Sonakshi and Kiera took off their jackets and tied them around their waists.

The surrounding bush had grown densely entwined and Sonakshi, in the back of her mind, noted that the birds had gone quiet. She rubbed her arms and listened more closely.

The tiny movements in the surrounding foliage, the rustling of rabbits in the bushes, the merry swaying of the branches of the trees—all the things she had become accustomed to for the last day—were now absent. She looked around anxiously and saw that although Kiera was walking along as normal, humming softly to her herself, Allira's eyes darted about into the trees and she twitched this way and that, looking at their surroundings, always on alert.

Allira noticed her looking, and Sonakshi gave her a troubled look.

Though it was more difficult to pick up on Allira's facial expressions given her snout, her eyes told Sonakshi the truth. Allira was worried, and Sonakshi couldn't take it anymore.

It was as if the very air had become heavy, pressing in on her. She stopped walking.

"Something's not right," she said.

Kiera swung around, eyes looking in all directions.

"What! What's happened?"

She looked at Allira. "You feel it too, don't you?"

Allira nodded quickly, ears bouncing.

"I just think the quicker we get out of this part of bush the better," said Allira.

Sonakshi nodded. "Alright, then let's go."

They jogged for a little while, Allira bounding along beside them, as the sun told them it was late afternoon.

"Help!" cried a panicked voice from far away.

The three of them stopped on the spot and stood stock still, listening.

"Stop, stop!" it came again. It was a boy's voice,

high-pitched and terrified, and coming from the bushland on the left of the track.

They exchanged looks of shock.

"What do we do?" asked Sonakshi.

"Nothing," said Kiera, "let's get out of here." She turned away.

But Sonakshi did not move.

Sonakshi *could not* move, to be exact. The scream she had heard held her in place.

That scream they had heard felt like it was sitting in her own throat.

And now there was no noise at all, and even the birds and beasts of the woodland had fallen silent, the way they only ever did in the face of a major, palpable threat. Sonakshi had a terrible feeling in her gut. She couldn't just leave it. She had to know what was going on.

"No," she said firmly. "It won't hurt to take a peek."

"It won't hurt?" hissed Kiera, "We might be next!"

"What if that were Rowen?"

Kiera gaped like a fish.

"I mean, wouldn't you want someone to go to Rowen if he was calling out for help?"

Kiera groaned. "I can't argue with that."

"We'll just *see* what's going on. It might be nothing."

In her heart, she knew that was not true. She just knew someone was being hurt out there.

The three of them left the path and went as quietly as they could into the bush on their left.

Stepping over branches and twigs and carefully

brushing away hanging leaves, they crept deeper into the bush. Sonakshi could hear more now.

There was a grunting and a snuffling, and heavy footsteps.

It did not take them long to reach the clearing where it was all happening. They huddled behind a bush and stared through. What they saw made their chests go tight.

A gigantic ape-like creature, at least seven feet tall, was pushing an old wheelbarrow in which a ginormous bird lay, a thick rope wrapped around its long skinny legs and elongated neck. It must have fainted from fear because it wasn't making any effort to resist its bonds.

The ape-man was made of muscle and dark, wiry hair, and, oddly, wore a pair of torn red shorts that barely fit. His powerful arms were incredibly long and almost reached the ground. His head was also like an ape's, with a broad nose and small but human-like eyes.

In the middle of the clearing was a circle of logs for sitting on, arranged neatly around a pile of firewood. And built around the firewood was a giant spit, used for roasting.

Two tall wooden spikes on either side balanced a long wooden pole between them.

"What is that?" whispered Kiera, her mouth hanging open in shock.

"An emu," said Allira breathlessly.

"No, what is *that* thing?"

Allira visibly gulped.

"We should go," she said. "That's—that's a Yowie."

The two girls stared at her.

"A Yow… a Yowie? What, the mystical Australian ape creature?" hissed Kiera, "I thought they were a joke!"

Sonakshi could not comment. They had conveniently missed that lesson with Dame Marie.

Allira looked at them and shook her head slowly. "They're very hard to find, as they keep to themselves mostly, but this one is a big guy. And he must be smart if he managed to get that wheelbarrow and clothes from someone. I suspect he didn't just ask nicely."

"Oh my God," said Kiera, looking back at the scene. "He's going to eat him! Poor thing!"

Sure enough, the Yowie was using the long piece of rope to tie the unconscious emu to the roasting spit, wrapping it around and around the emu's torso.

"Let's go," said Allira, turning. "I can't watch."

But Sonakshi grabbed Allira's arm. She could not get out of her head how much the voice had sounded like Rowen, afraid and helpless. She couldn't just let him get eaten.

"We're not going to watch it," she said with finality. "We're going to *stop* it."

"What?" hissed Allira. "That's just an emu."

"And are you just a kangaroo? We all heard it speak."

Allira fell silent.

"Geez," grumbled Kiera under her breath, "how many talking wildlife are there?"

A small grunt drew their attention back to the Yowie. He had hoisted the emu onto the spit and now began fiddling with the pieces of wood below the suspended body.

From their position, they watched in horror as Yowie took hold of a book of matches and was attempting to light one. But his huge fingers couldn't properly grasp the tiny wooden sticks and one snapped in half, slipping from his fingers and dropping to the dirt.

The Yowie roared in frustration, throwing his head back in the air, exposing a mouth full of giant yellow canines that looked incredibly sharp.

The girls recoiled from the noise and clapped their hands over their ears.

"Okay," whispered Kiera. "I don't know how long it's going to take for him to figure out how to light that thing, but how exactly are you planning on rescuing that emu?"

"Please, can we just go?" pleaded Allira. "I mean—"

But a squawk cut her off. The emu had woken up and was wriggling in its bindings.

"Hey!" it shouted, "let me go!"

The Yowie jumped up with a grunt and grabbed a pile of sticks from the ground, shoving them inside the emu's mouth. The giant bird gave a muffled squawk of protest, but they couldn't make out any words. But a single tear rang down its cheek and dropped into the dirt. The Yowie sniffed and went back to the matches.

That swayed Allira completely. She had never seen a bird cry tears before, for one thing.

"How should we do this, Sonakshi?" asked Allira. "Like you said, we can't leave him."

"Okay, here's what I'm thinking."

Sonakshi gave them her idea. In her mind, it was rather simple. But the other two looked uncertainly at each other.

"A lot could go wrong," said Allira.

"Yes, and we don't have any way to predict his reaction," said Kiera.

"We'll just have to go with it," Sonakshi said. In the back of her mind, she knew what could go wrong. The risk was a big one. But it was also a calculated one. Due to their many years sneaking around the castle, Sonakshi and Kiera had become very good at being stealthy.

She looked at the Yowie sitting with his matches in hand. He looked heavy. Her mother had always said that there was a way to plan for everything… it seemed as though making the risky decision to leave home had given Sonakshi a spurt of confidence and inspiration.

And somehow, she knew they could pull this off.

This Yowie couldn't be any cleverer than Captain Sampson or Dame Marie, and the girls managed to trick those two all the time. In fact, tricking them was so easy it was boring.

"Alright," she said. "It's now or never. Kiera, grab the camping knife from our bags, as you'll need to be the one to cut him loose."

Kiera rummaged through her bag, producing the silver blade. She gripped it firmly as Sonakshi nodded her head at her and Allira.

"Remember," Sonakshi whispered, "Be ready to run

back the way we came and down the path." They both nodded seriously.

Sonakshi crept silently along the line of trees, circling the Yowie on the side his back was facing. She needed to be on the side of clearing as far away as possible from the emu. It was late afternoon now, and the sunset would soon make the clearing dark.

When she reached the point farthest from the campfire, she stepped backwards, farther into the shadows. Quickly and silently, she turned into her unicorn form.

"Hello!" she called.

The Yowie jumped up in surprise and turned, staring into the trees.

Sonakshi moved farther back into the forest, making a loud rustling sound.

Through the trees, behind the Yowie, she could see Allira and Kiera creeping towards the campfire. The Yowie stepped forward, sniffing the air suspiciously, his long arms swaying irritably by his side. He looked curious but also confused.

"Here!" she shouted.

The Yowie cocked his head as if listening but did not move a step farther. Behind him, Allira and Kiera had reached the emu and were staring at the back of the Yowie, wide-eyed.

He then started to turn back towards the emu. It was time to act.

Sonakshi charged through the forest towards the Yowie, and stunned by the noise, he stopped turning. She broke through the security of the trees and came to a halt a short distance from him. Kiera took the opportunity to take the knife to the ropes and began furiously cutting.

The Yowie stared at Sonakshi with eyes like dinner plates.

"Hello," she said boldly. "How are you?"

It was a very strange introduction, one that served well to confuse the giant ape man.

He stared at her transfixed, his gazed moving from her hooves all the way up to her horn.

"Unicorn," he breathed in a heavy, gravelly voice.

"Yes," she whispered, a bit surprised herself.

It was working, the Yowie was captivated.

But it appeared all was not going to plan. Allira, for some reason, had broken away from Kiera and the emu, and was now creeping away from the fire. Sonakshi panicked.

What is she doing? She had to keep the Yowie occupied.

"Who are you?" she asked softly.

He whispered something in a language she didn't understand.

"Yowie?" she asked uncertainly.

He shook his head vigorously, said a strange, harsh word, and swiped his palm in the air in a cutting motion.

"You don't like that name. I do apologise. What name do you like to go by?"

He looked totally captivated now— somehow he knew what she was and wanted to talk to her.

He made the cutting gesture a second time, and

followed up with something in his grunting language. So, he *really* hated the name Yowie.

Now, Allira was crouching down, off to the side.

Sonakshi did not dare not look directly at her.

"How many of you are there?" she asked him. "Do you have a family here?"

His head cocked to one side, then swung to the other side, listening to her speak.

Then he answered just as softly in reply, but his tone was sad.

"Just you then?" Sonakshi guessed, stepping forward, to make sure his attention stayed on her. But he only had eyes for her anyway. The clearing was getting darker and her horn glowed. She could see it in the reflection of his pupils. It seemed he was enthralled by her.

"You're just like me, then," she said. "I think I'm the only one too."

He swayed, as if in a trance. She kept going, keeping her voice soft.

"You are admiring my horn? I like it too; it's very powerful."

From the side of her eye, she saw the emu plop to the ground, Kiera and Allira were now trying to unravel him from the remaining rope. It was a real struggle and the bird was hardly compliant.

But the Yowie didn't seem to notice all the shuffling noises behind him.

"Yes, sometimes, I wonder if I'm the only one too. And I ask myself what it would be like if I knew another unicorn. Do you ever think how it would be to know another…like you?"

She had almost slipped up and used the word Yowie again. But she stopped herself in time.

The Yowie nodded slowly, and Sonakshi was sure she saw loneliness in his eyes, the pain and sadness of being the only creature of his kind. But she also felt a strong will to live and hope. The only thing you could do as the only one was to keep going, never giving up.

"I'm sorry," she said, and she wasn't even sure why.

And then everything changed.

The Emu gave a loud squawk of pain. And Kiera cried out, "Sorry!"

The Yowie spun around and seeing his treasure on the ground, roared, lunging towards them. The emu sprang to his feet and ran toward the forest behind, Allira and Kiera scrambling after him. "No!" cried Sonakshi, running behind the Yowie.

But the Yowie took a step and stumbled, falling face-first on the ground.

"Be careful, Sona!" cried Allira from the tree line. "I set up a snare!"

Sonakshi almost tripped over the Yowie, but caught herself just in time. He cried out, clutching at his foot, a tight band of rope cutting into it.

"I'm so sorry!" Sonakshi cried, running past him and joining Kiera and Allira as they hurtled into the forest behind the emu. They had only gone a short way when they found the big bird fallen over in the dirt, the last parts of the rope tangled about his spindly legs.

Kiera and Allira jumped to help him.

"Let go of me!" the emu cried.

"We're trying to help you, you dingbat!" cried Kiera, releasing him and throwing the tangle of rope aside. The Yowie roared again behind them.

"A likely story!" he cried, running towards the main trail.

"The snare won't hold him long," panted Allira. "He'll be on us in a second!"

Sure enough, the sound of heavy feet through the forest belted at them.

Allira immediately bolted.

"Get on my back!" cried Sonakshi, coming over to Kiera.

Kiera did not argue and clambered upon Sonakshi's bare back, bags in hand. Sonakshi lurched forward and accelerated into a full gallop behind Allira.

The Yowie's shouts rapidly faded away as Sonakshi leapt through the forest, dodging hanging tree limbs and jumping over large bushes, praying the main road would appear soon.

Sure enough, they broke free of the forest and turned left down the road, where they could see the shadow of Allira pursuing the Emu in the distance.

There were no faster animals in the world across a flat road than an emu, a kangaroo, and a unicorn; even with Kiera on her back, there was no way the heavy Yowie could catch them.

In the back of her mind, Sonakshi thought with amusement that if she had to choose animals to go with her on a chase, these would be the ones she'd select. What luck.

They ran and bounded and galloped for kilometers.

All the while, Sonakshi kept the emu within her line of sight. After what seemed like half an hour of running at full speed, she thought it was time to slow down and stop. They would be wrecked otherwise, and the emu must have been running on full adrenaline.

No way did anyone have that much energy.

Then again, she thought, they were running from almost certain death.

Sonakshi, even with Kiera riding on her back, was the fastest, so when she sped up, she caught up to the other two after a few moments as Kiera held on for dear life.

She raced in front of the emu and cut him off from the front, Allira closing in from behind.

The emu skidded to a stop, so shocked by the sight of a Unicorn, he almost bumped into them. "Stop!" said Sonakshi. "We don't mean you harm."

"You're a unicorn!" he said in disbelief.

"Yeah."

"Well, leave me alone!" he said angrily, pacing back and forth, looking for an exit.

"We did save you just now, sir," said Kiera in an unimpressed tone.

"Yes, I guess so, thanks for that."

"So what's your name?" asked Kiera.

"Why do you want to know that?" asked the emu suspiciously.

Kiera rolled her eyes, retorting, "because that's what you do when you meet people. You introduce yourself. It's good manners!"

When the emu only frowned at her, Kiera sighed with exasperation.

"Well let me go first. I'm Lady Kiera of Cabbage Tree Creek, and this is... Her Royal Highness Sonakshi the Unicorn Princess, and that's Allira the kangaroo. I don't see any point in hiding it anymore." She gave Sonakshi a half-shrug.

The emu's eyes widened and he opened his beak, then closed it. Then he did this again.

"I- Um. Well." He fluffed his feathers irritably. "My name is Miro."

"We shall call you Miro the Grump," said Kiera with finality, "Because that is what you are."

"Kiera!" said Sonakshi with surprise.

Kiera shrugged. "My mother told me to always speak the truth."

Miro fluffed his wings again. "Well!"

Kiera slid off Sonakshi and gave her a look to say, *see, I told you he was grumpy.*

"You must be tired after all the running," said Sonakshi. "We've run kilometers. I don't think I can run anymore. Do you want to camp with us for tonight?"

"What about the Yowie?" he asked.

"We've run so far, there's no way *anyone* could catch up to us tonight."

"Fine. I will stay with you for some time," said Miro in a dull voice. "Safety in numbers."

"Yes, I would agree," said Sonakshi kindly. "We are travelling to the other side of the forest."

Miro nodded regally and followed them until they

found a patch of grass away from the road to rest on. Miro looked very impressed when he saw Sonakshi change back into her human form for the night. They toasted rolls over a campfire and Miro filled them in about how he had been travelling through the bush, returning from visiting his aunt when the Yowie ambushed him. They did not bother to ask him why he could talk.

In return, he didn't bother to ask them questions either.

They went to sleep in silence that night, all too shocked and tired to make small talk.

Sonakshi closed her eyes, listening to the cicadas around them. Her mind went back to the small, yet intelligent eyes of the Yowie. He was all alone back there, he'd said. Yet she was sure Dame Marie had mentioned that there was more than one Yowie around. They were so good at hiding themselves from the rest of the world that they were hidden from each other!

Could it be the same for unicorns?

Could it be that she'd been so cooped up in her hiding place in the valley that she had missed out on knowing others just like her? All she knew was she did not want to end up like that Yowie, alone in the forest and munching on the only potential friends that came his way.

No, she was glad to have met Allira—lucky, even.

Without her, they would be completely lost in this vast bushland.

And she'd even listened to Sonakshi when she asked

Allira not to mention her to her mother in the letter. Still, a tinge of sadness was still hanging around Allira.

She must miss her mum quite a lot, as she sure wrote to her daily, sometimes more.

What a day, Sonakshi thought before sleep took her, *if we make this a habit, we'll have collected the whole forest's animals before we reach Freshwater Bay!*

CHAPTER TEN

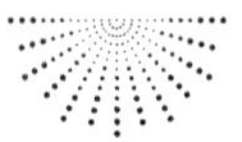

Over the decades, I have learned two things about finding a unicorn. The first is that to find one, you must follow a specific series of steps not known to many men. The second is to forget your pursuit of finding a unicorn foal. Man learning flight is more likely to happen.
—Lord Andrew Godfrey, *The Annals of Unicorn Sightings of the 16th Century, 1701.*

They woke the next morning to find Miro sitting glumly by the dying fire. The girls exchanged a look before packing away their sleeping bags.

"What's your deal, Miro?" asked Kiera, coming to sit next to him. "Not a morning person?"

"Not generally, no," he replied, "especially after almost getting cooked alive by a Yowie."

Kiera rolled her eyes at Sonakshi and then frowned

when she realised Sonakshi was not paying attention. She was rummaging urgently through their food bag.

"Have you lost something?" asked Kiera.

"In a way…" Her voice trailed off. "Were those bread rolls we ate last night the last ones?"

Kiera came over, looking pale.

She took the bag, turned it upside down and shook it. Nothing came out.

"Was there another bag?" Sonakshi asked nervously.

Kiera gulped, her face twisting into a pained expression.

Sonakshi's heart sank into her chest. They had eaten all the food.

From his log by the fire, Miro made an unimpressed sound and fluffed his wings.

"New to travelling, are we?" he said darkly. "Rookie error."

Kiera rounded on him, furious.

"If you don't have anything nice to say, don't say anything at all!"

Miro pursed his giant beak but said nothing.

"What do we do now?" asked Kiera, looking around them as if scones and Danishes would appear growing on the trees at any moment.

"Learn to eat worms and insects?" asked Miro dryly. "They're tasty once you get used to it and you'll never run out."

Kiera gasped in disgust. "Never! You're a disturbed person… umm…bird!"

Miro opened his beak in shock. "*Disturbed?* This is

native bush food! Everyone around here eats it! And as for *bird thing*—"

"But I'm human, Miro! I need human food!"

"Oh, come on. Humans used to eat this stuff all the time. Hunter-gatherers. They lived off whatever they could find. You're just spoiled."

"Well!" said Kiera, crossing her arms and dumping herself down on the log opposite him, her lips pursed. "Well, I can't argue with that. But you should be nicer to me. I did free you after all and I'm beginning to wonder why!"

"Yes, you saved me, and you stabbed me while you were at it!"

"I did say sorry, you oversized chicken!"

"I thought you said you were a lady."

"Stop it you two!" cried Sonakshi, thoroughly annoyed. "We need to sort out this problem."

Allira came over to join them, closing her bag.

"Where were you?" asked Miro suspiciously.

She looked up at him in shock.

"I was writing to my mother if you *must* know," she said, somewhat defensive.

Miro flapped his wings as if he had just heard the most irritating thing being said to him.

"And I have—" Allira reached into her pouch, rummaged around and pulled out three objects. "—Three carrots left!" She held them out, and the girls took one each with thanks.

"Thank you Allira," said Kiera, giving Miro a pointed look. "Thank you for sharing. Miro, just because one Yowie kidnapped you, there's no reason to be suspicious of everybody!"

"Er—No problem," said Allira quickly. "I'm sure we'll find food somehow. We're in a forest after all," she looked around, appearing thoughtful. "There have to be lots of fruits and vegetables we can eat around here."

Sonakshi finished her carrot in one bite.

"I can't believe you ate all the food, Kiera," grumbled Sonakshi.

"*Me?*" cried Kiera. "You ate just as much as I did!"

"Rubbish! You ate twice as much as I did. This entire time." Then she put on a high-pitched voice, imitating Kiera, *It's two rolls for me, and one roll for you, Sona.*

"That's rubbish!"

"And you were always taking the food from under my bed. I hardly got to eat any!"

"I saw you take two rolls last night," said Miro.

"See!"

"Oh, gang up on me then!" cried Kiera, close to tears. "You two go and be best friends!"

She turned on her heel and stormed off into the trees.

Sonakshi stood up angrily to pursue her, but Allira put a hand on her shoulder.

"Let her go cool off. She'll come back when she's ready."

Sonakshi sat back down, her stomach grumbling. Why did Kiera always do this? She *never* thought ahead, and was always going off, doing things whenever she liked.

Sonakshi shook herself and thought of their current situation.

"We ran so far last night. Do you think we'll be close to Freshwater Bay?"

"Oh hmm," said Miro. "So that's where you're going, is it? There might be another three days of walking if I'm honest."

"Well," said Sonakshi, "We'll just have to deal with it. They'll surely have food on the boat."

"You're catching a boat?" asked Miro.

Sonakshi groaned internally. Her big mouth! She had might as well tell the world where they were going.

She nodded at him, but remained silent. Miro looked from her to Allira and their bags. She could almost see the gears turning in his brain, trying to figure out what two young girls were doing in the forest alone with Allira. Sonakshi quickly started a conversation with the beautiful kangaroo, asking her about her family.

Sure enough, half an hour later, Kiera stomped back into the campsite and grabbed her backpack, not making eye contact with anyone.

And so they continued back on the road, trudging alone, in quietness.

By midday, however, Sonakshi's hunger made her anger dissipate and everybody heard Kiera's tummy grumbling loudly.

"Guys, I really need some food," she said desperately.

"Kiera," said Miro impatiently, "I told you to try—"

"I will not eat worms!" cried Kiera angrily. "I'll vomit!"

"What are you going to do then, huh?"

The group stopped in their tracks as Allira bounded off to a nearby bush. When she came back, she held a small pile of tiny pink berries.

"Here," she said, pouring them into Kiera's waiting hands, "I've seen bush berries growing here every so often."

Kiera popped one in her mouth and chewed. "Ywwweck!" She spat it out and vigorously wiped her tongue on her sleeve. "It's so bitter!" she cried, "Allira, you've poisoned me!"

Allira and Miro laughed. "It's not poisonous," Allira said. "It's just not sweet."

"Well, *I* can't eat them."

"Thanks for trying," said Sonakshi to Allira. "Is there any more bush food we can try?"

"Hmm," thought Allira, "Maybe some tubers? We can cook them up over a fire for lunch."

"That sounds good," said Sonakshi, "and we brought a saucepan with us."

And so they went along down the road and Allira, who seemed to be an expert in picking out potential edible plants, eventually found a group of long, leafy plants that she thought looked promising.

She and Kiera knelt in the dry grass and dug up the plants. And with a cry of surprise, Kiera lifted one up to show a small round potato growing from the bottom.

"Who do you think planted this potato here?" she asked, excitedly.

"No one," said Miro, unimpressed. "It's just a bush potato, it grows naturally."

Kiera stared at it in wonder while Allira and Sonakshi dug up a few more that had been growing together. Miro watched on glumly, as with no hands, he couldn't really help. The strong claws on his feet were not useful to them either, as they would tear the plants to shreds.

Once they had four tiny potatoes tucked safely into their food bag, they walked until they found a spot to set up a campfire. Kiera's tummy grumbled loudly again, and looking miserably at the tiny potato that would be hers, she started a fire and put a pot of water to boil over it.

They cleaned the potatoes as best they could and put them in the water.

Then they all sat around the fire and watched the pot.

After fifteen minutes, Kiera poked a fork into one of them to see if they were cooked.

"It's done!" she cried happily, "They're soft!"

She dished them out into a bowl and waited for them to cool for five minutes before handing them out. Sonakshi took hers and saw how tiny it was.

It sat warm in her palm, tiny but smelling great.

Kiera put hers into her mouth whole. Chewing slowly, she made a face.

"Shame we don't have any salt or rosemary," she said thickly.

"It's lovely," said Sonakshi. And it was partially true, since anything, even a tiny, bland bush potato would taste good to a hungry tummy.

"Well," said Miro haughtily. "That's lunch done then."

They packed up their campfire and set out again, but Sonakshi did not miss the sad look on Kiera's face. They had to be reaching Freshwater Bay soon, she thought, and she was not sure how long Kiera would last surviving on sour bush berries and miniature potatoes.

And with all the moaning Kiera was doing, it seemed she must have been hoping for a five-starred restaurant just around the next bend.

They continued down the road for the rest of that day, all keeping an eye out for any more bush potatoes. But hours passed, and they found none. The sky changed colour above them, signalling the day was wearing on, and soon, it was telling them it was late afternoon.

It would be night again soon, and they still had found nothing to eat.

They went to bed with hungry tummies that night, except Miro, who found 'some tasty worms' which he ate well away from the group upon Kiera's demand.

The next day, they travelled through the forest. Kiera and Miro bickered and fought over tiny things such as the exact color of a tree or the diet of a wombat. They found another batch of tiny potatoes, which seemed to only make Kiera more upset. Nothing ever pleased her!

She was becoming impossible, and pulling down the rest of the group.

She walked quietly, looking so upset that even Miro did not comment.

And he also did not, as Sonakshi noticed, say anything about his plans to leave them. Perhaps he was quite shaken up by the Yowie and didn't want to leave the safety of the group.

Twilight came, and Sonakshi was about to say that they should think about finding a sleeping spot when something marvellous happened.

They smelled it in the air first. It was the unmistakable and scrumptious smell of a cooked dinner, wafting towards them on the slight breeze. Kiera lifted her nose in the air and sniffed.

"It smells like…. pizza!" She gave another sniff, "And freshly baked cinnamon muffins!"

It was the first time anyone had seen a smile on Kiera's face in a long while.

Allira sniffed too, her long nose flaring. "I can smell roasted carrots!"

"You don't think its wishful thinking?" said Miro snidely, with narrowed eyes, but he sniffed the air keenly, too. And then they rounded a sharp corner and saw it.

All four of them, even Miro, gasped in shock.

A fenced field of lush green trees grew on the left-hand side of the path. Most notably, from the trees, however, grew… "Muffins?" asked Kiera with awe.

She shot towards the hip-high fence, then leaned over and stared at the closest trees.

"Sona!" she cried, pointing. "Guys! Look, it's a muffin tree!"

The group came to join her at the fence, staring at the trees in wonder.

"Impossible," breathed Miro. "Muffins don't grow on trees."

"Is that… a blueberry Danish hanging from that branch there?" asked Sonakshi, frowning.

"But that can't be a croissant dangling—can it?"

A golden waffle dropped to the ground with a soft thump, evidently ready to eat. They all breathed in sharply. It sat there in the lush green grass, enticing them with its crispy curves.

"Do you think we're hallucinating?" asked Allira. "Like one of those mirages in a desert?"

"Hmm," was all Miro said.

"Well, it can't be, because I can smell it," said Kiera, wiping her mouth. "But there's only one way to find out."

She put a foot on the bottom rung of the wooden fence.

"I don't think that's a good idea," said Miro.

"Why?" asked Kiera, swinging herself across. She landed on the bright green grass on the other side and raised her hands up in the air in a flourish.

"There are so many here," she said, turning to look at the nearest tree. "Taking one or two won't hurt the trees."

"It's not the trees I'm worried about," Miro said, coming to the fence next to Sonakshi. "Look at this fence. It's newly painted and well cared for, so I'll hazard a guess that someone doesn't want people going in."

"And the land is enormous," said Allira. "This fence goes so far down the road I can't even see where it finishes. And these plants do look very well-tended. Maybe we should ask the owner first? Shall we go to see if we can find him?"

But Kiera was not listening.

Her nose and her famished gut seemed to be leading the way.

She began wandering into the trees, oblivious to everyone's cries, and a small collection of pastries suddenly grew in her hands. She stared at them, wide-eyed.

"Sona! It smells so good in here, come in!"

But Sonakshi hesitated. Her tummy was grumbling, sure, but this fence gave her reason to pause. If it was someone's property, they couldn't just take what they wanted. This was just not the polite way in which she'd been brought up. Her parents had taught Sonakshi to treat everything with respect when it belonged to someone else. She cringed, watching Kiera.

But Kiera only went farther into the yard where they could not see her.

"Kiera!" Miro called, "Don't go that far in! Come back!"

Suddenly, they heard her gasp again, even farther away now.

And Sonakshi wanted to jump over the fence and go get her to come back.

"Everyone!" Kiera called, "You've got to see this! Come in! It's all okay!"

Sonakshi, Allira and Miro exchanged uncertain glances. In the end, Sonakshi was not comfortable having Kiera wander off on her own. So she shrugged her shoulders to her friends and clambered over the fence.

"Come on over guys; I don't want us to get separated."

Grumbling and unsure, both Miro and Allira obliged, jumping over the fence.

"Hmm, it sure does smell good in here," said Allira, staring up at the tree with little cakes hanging from the branches.

Miro reached his long neck to sniff a strawberry pastry hanging low off a branch.

"Hmm." He said, narrowing his eyes.

The three of them walked through the little forest of trees until they found Kiera.

It appeared that she had found the savoury section.

Savoury pies, sausage rolls, and mushroom pizzas hung from these trees and the aroma was incredible. Sonakshi closed her mouth, worried she would be drooling all over herself if she didn't. Her tummy grumbled hopefully, and her eyes were big and round.

"Sona, you have to grow these trees back at the palace!" said Kiera, reaching for a slice of pizza. "Imagine, pastries and muffins on demand! I'd be the size of a house!"

She took a bite and a look of bliss covered her face as she chewed.

"Oh my gosh!" she said happily, mouth full. "You have to try this! It's so good!"

She gobbled it down quickly and took another slice off the branch.

"Try this, Sona." She held out the cheesy slice for Sonakshi to taste.

She reluctantly accepted a bite of the pizza. Flavour exploded in her mouth. There was cheese and rich sauce, rosemary, and fragrant tomatoes. Boy, was it good.

"You're right, Kiera, I've tasted nothing like it."

A twig snapped behind them.

"Oh hello there," came an unfamiliar female voice.

Sonakshi jumped and flashed into her unicorn form in shock. All four of them spun around to a beautiful blonde woman in a long, green embroidered dress smiling at them pleasantly. She was holding a wicker basket full of pastries. Her bright blue eyes sparkled, looking at them each in turn, not seeming to notice Sonakshi had transformed into a unicorn in front of her.

"Oh, hi," said Kiera, a little stuck for words as flakes of pastry dropped from her chin.

"Who are you?" asked Miro rudely.

"I see you have found Emily's Garden. I am Emily." She pointed to herself, walking towards them. "Please, you look exhausted and hungry. So, do eat. Have you travelled far?"

"Yes," said Kiera, pushing between Allira and Miro. "We are so starved. I'm sorry, I just tried one of the pizzas. It was heavenly…"

Emily beamed at her, looking her up and down.

"Please, eat more, as much as you need."

"That is very kind of you," said Sonakshi. "We can pay you for it."

Kiera brought out some gold coins from their bags and offered them to Emily.

It was only Miro who noticed the way Emily's eyes followed Kiera's every movement, or the way her eyes widened when she saw the gold.

"No, no!" said Emily, "I do not need your payment. The look of enjoyment on your faces is enough for me. Emily's Garden exists to help all travellers on their way."

She offered Allira her basket.

"Have you tried any yet? The carrot cake is my favourite."

Allira's eyes widened as she accepted the carrot cake.

"Wow," she said, chewing. "It's great."

"Can I tempt you?" asked Emily to Miro. "These berry Danishes are exquisite."

"Sure," said Miro in an oddly cheerful voice and allowed Emily to place the Danish directly into his beak. He threw back his head and looked as if he gulped it down.

The eaten pastry globs, however, were not visible as lumps descending his long neck. Instead, his cheeks became puffed out.

"Come," said Emily. "You must be tired of standing, let us sit down and chat together."

Emily revealed a large purple picnic blanket she had

been keeping in the crook of her arm. She laid it out carefully so it would fit all of them. Sonakshi, still in unicorn form, sat on her belly on the side of the blanket.

"Where are you from?" she asked when they were all seated and chewing happily.

"The other side of the forest," said Sonakshi.

"We're headed to the Bay," finished Kiera.

"Really?" drawled Emily slowly. "How wonderful. Please, eat more."

She offered a chocolate tart to Kiera, who took it happily.

"Do you think we'll be able to take some for our travels, Emily?" asked Kiera. "We ran out of food, you see."

"Oh dear!" cried Emily dramatically. "What a horrible situation!"

She patted Kiera on the arm. "Have no fear, dear, I will give you plenty."

"That is very nice of you," said Allira, yawning widely.

"Oh Allira, you've started me yawning too!" said Kiera. "Though I could go for nap just about now."

"Yes, I'm feeling rather sleepy too," Sonakshi said.

Allira already had her eyes closed.

"Lie down in this soft blanket," said Emily gently. "You'll find that it's very comfortable."

Kiera and Allira lay down, and Sonakshi put her head down, allowing it to rest on her front hooves. After a moment, Miro too closed his eyes.

As the heavy magical sleeping spell took over his

friends, Miro was glad he had listened to his instincts. Perhaps the Yowie had made him distrustful of everybody, but he had only pretended to eat this food, spitting it out behind him where Emily couldn't see.

He closed his beady black eyes and let his head fall forwards. He had to keep up the act.

Kiera and Allira fell asleep as soon as their heads hit the ground.

Just before Sonakshi fell asleep, she saw Emily's beautiful face morph, but she was too sleepy to even say anything. Emily's eyes grew far apart, and hair and boils sprouted from her formerly smooth skin, and the nose grew longer and became hooked.

One of her beautiful eyes disappeared completely, replaced by wrinkly brown skin.

'Emily' was now a grumpy-looking man.

He snarled at Sonakshi and bared his yellow rotten teeth.

Fear laced through her, but the pull of sleep was far too strong. She fought it, but her eyelids closed of their own accord.

"A unicorn," she heard him mutter in a deep, rough voice, very different from the one he'd had just moments before. "This must be my lucky day. Look at that sparkling horn. Worth a pretty penny, indeed…"

CHAPTER ELEVEN

Heavy it rests on the shoulders of a unicorn, the responsibility of being loved by all.
—Lord Andrew Godfrey, *The Annals of Unicorn Sightings of the 16th Century, 1701.*

Miro lay as still as he could as the scarred, one-eyed man took out a walkie talkie from his pocket. "Hello Gary?" he said, rough voice dripping with glee. "Yeah, I got me a full-grown unicorn! Would you believe it! Gotta be worth a bit."

Miro could not hear the mumbled reply through all the crackling and static of the walkie talkie, but he could hear Gary on the other side exclaim with surprise and excitement.

"Yep, would you believe it! And there's some wildlife and one human girl. Come and bring the cart, soon as you can. We'll load 'em in."

Miro couldn't believe what he had witnessed.

As the beautiful lady Emily stooped over Princess Sonakshi, she had transformed before his very eyes into a cruel-looking man with one beady looking eye.

He looked rather ridiculous prancing around the clearing in that green dress, but there was still something sinister about that man, so Miro didn't feel much mirth at the sight.

The ugly, wizened stranger had drugged them and was now planning to take them away somewhere. By the looks of it, he seemed to have done this before. Whatever he was planning to do with them all would not be good. This was all greedy Kiera's fault; if she hadn't trespassed into the muffin trees, none of this would ever have come to pass! But thinking about this didn't help. If there was something he knew for sure, it was that he did not escape from the Yowie just to have them all be made captive again. Miro's heart pounded fast.

They didn't have to wait long for the noisy rumbling sound of the cart and horse to arrive with 'Gary'. Miro cracked an eye open from his position on the ground and saw two pairs of brown sneakers walking towards them all, scuffing at the dirt as they went.

"Look at her, Glen!" said the new voice, Gary. "Beautiful, she'll fetch a nifty price."

"She sure will! And the others we can chop up and feed to lions, out back. No one will know they ever existed when those cats are done with 'em."

Lions! Miro thought. *First a Yowie and now lions. I have to get out of this forsaken forest.*

There were grunting noises and the sound of something heavy being hoisted upwards.

Miro cracked his eyes open again and saw they were lifting Allira into the back of the wooden cart. The men turned and came back, discussing how they would lift the unicorn.

"We'll put the others in first," said the one-eyed man, "And then we'll hoist the unicorn up using the blanket. We might even need to attach her to the cart and drag her."

I can't believe it! Miro thought as they lifted Allira up. *They saved me from imprisonment, and now we will* all *be prisoners ourselves! I'll be a prisoner again. I won't have it, I won't.*

In one sweeping movement, Miro rose from the ground, got his bearings by looking left and right, and bolted through the trees to then leap right over the fence.

"Oi!" came a shout from behind him. But Miro had already cleared the fence.

And then he ran and ran and ran.

"Don't worry about it, Gary," said Glen. "He's long gone by now. Anyway, he's not the one we want. What would we do with a hulking great bird? Except eat it—and I ain't that hungry."

Sonakshi woke up feeling horrible. She was sore all over. It felt as though someone had dragged her body over rough rocks for kilometers. When she rolled over and opened her eyes, she realised that someone had done that very thing. She was still on the picnic rug from yesterday.

The first thing she saw was that it was very dark. It felt as if it was late into the night.

But there were rows and rows of metal bars all around her.

Oh no, she thought. *Oh no, oh no, oh no!*

She looked to her right and saw her cage was in a sheltered area next to a large brick building. And then she looked to her left and cried out with dismay as she saw Kiera's crumpled body lying on the concrete in her own separate cage. She stirred just slightly.

"Whoa!" Kiera's voice was groggy. She lifted her head and shakily got onto her knees.

The delicious food, Sonakshi thought. *He drugged the food on the trees.*

She realised now: Emily wasn't who she appeared to be!

"Sona! Kiera!" came a shrill but familiar voice from farther away. Sonakshi craned her head to look past Kiera's cage. On the other side, Allira pressed her face against the bars between Kiera's and her own cage. Sonakshi got up onto her hooves with difficulty.

She groaned, feeling that her body must be full of bruises.

"Allira! Are you okay?" she asked. "Emily is not who she said!"

"I'm okay! Just sleepy," said Allira, "That food was no good."

"It made us go to sleep," said Sonakshi darkly. "How could we have been so stupid?"

"We were hungry," said Allira. "The only problem is, I can't see Miro. Is he by your side?"

Sonakshi looked around, but all she could see were the brick walls of the building.

No other souls in sight. And everything was quiet and still.

"He's not here. Where could he be?"

"I—" Allira hesitated. "I saw him spit out the food."

"Oh, clever Miro," said Kiera. "He could've warned us though."

"This is all your fault," said Sonakshi quietly, eyeing Kiera with a quick glance, as if she would rather not look her full on in the face. The look said, *you could have killed us all.*

Kiera turned to look at her.

"All my fault? It's not though..."

"Yes! If you hadn't gone and jumped over the fence, like we'd all told you—"

"But you all followed me! I didn't drag you there!"

"I followed because I didn't want you going into danger alone!"

"Don't lie, you were hungry too!"

"If it wasn't for you, we wouldn't be locked up. We wouldn't have been poisoned."

"Stop it!" Allira shouted.

The two girls halted. Kiera turned away from Sonakshi.

"Focus, you two. Arguing will only make us weaker, and better prey for them. So just stop it. Anyway, what do you think they want to do with us?"

"We have to get out of here," said Sonakshi

She checked around her cage. All their bags and equipment were gone.

"Sona..." said Allira slowly. "I heard something before."

"What was it?"

"Well, I..." She broke off and looked down, as if the words were hard to say. "I swear I heard a lion roar."

"They have *lions* here?" asked Sonakshi incredulously. "No! Maybe you were imagining things. You know, under the influence of the poison."

Kiera tutted loudly. "Stop calling it poison. We're all alive, aren't we?"

"No thanks to you," spat Sonakshi, her blood pressure soaring sky high as she listened to Kiera's constant attempts to evade any blame or acknowledge this was her fault.

"I said shut up! Stop fighting!" cried Allira, her paws flattening her little ears. "I said there are lions here, and all you two can do is fight and bicker."

"So... lions?" Sonakshi whispered, as if by keeping a low voice, the lions might turn out to be just a dream.

But Allira nodded, wide-eyed, and heart's palpitations visible through her soft brown fur. Kiera looked scared too, sitting in her cage with her arms crossed, staring off into space.

Sonakshi didn't reply. She simply stared at the metal bars in thought.

She was still in her unicorn form, and briefly wondered if she should change back into her human form—and decided against it. It was better if they just thought she was a random unicorn wandering the forest, rather than an actual princess too.

They might end up holding her for ransom just as Mankini was doing with Rowen!

No, she had to get out of here. She wondered briefly about Miro and whether he was safely out of the forest by now. They couldn't have been far from the Bay, and she counted the days in her head. One night, two nights… this was their third night! They were supposed to get to Freshwater Bay by the fourth day! If they didn't board the ship Mankini had sent for them tomorrow, they were done for. Or at least, Rowen was done for. She paced around her small cage looking for their options, searching for some clue that would enable them to escape. She really wished she had her lock picks with her. Or a bobby pin!

That would be enough!

And she remembered she had some in her hair as a human.

But she didn't get the chance to change forms because just then, two scraggly men appeared from around the corner. She recognised one because he wore the same green dress Emily had worn. They looked like twins except the other brother had both his eyes, and wore regular men's clothes. This one came forward, waving a small piece of paper in his hand.

"Well, well, well!" he said, "Roo, we found this in

your bag. If we'd have known you were a friend of Mankini, then we wouldn't have caged you!"

Kiera jumped up and ran to the bars, flinging herself against the cold metal as if she would break the massive, thick bars in two, so panicked was she. At the same time, Sonakshi felt as if her whole body became frozen on the spot. *Friend of Mankini? Friend of Mankini!*

"What's going on?" cried Kiera, grabbing the bars. "Please, please, let me out!"

She had become hysterical, inconsolable, and she was deeply, deeply scared.

The man in the green dress brought out a set of keys and unlocked Allira's cage.

Allira looked between the men, then to Kiera and Sonakshi, and did not move.

He held the cage door wide open.

"Yeah, sorry about that. Well, what are you waiting for, you're free."

"Yes, any friend of Mankini's is a friend of ours. Come on out, Roo!" said the second man.

Sonakshi looked at the letter in the second man's big hand, and she looked at Allira.

And then it all made sense. Allira had been following them. She had been writing letters and had been very keen to join in with their trip. And she, Sonakshi, had been blind to it.

"I—I…." Allira bounded out of the cage and turned to look at the girls.

"How could you!" cried Kiera, her red hair flapping. "You were writing to Mankini, spying on us? You are disgusting!"

Sonakshi stood speechless.

"I'm sorry..."

Allira couldn't find her words and the man with the letter patted her on the back.

"You were our friend," said Sonakshi softly. "I thought we could trust you."

"We are so stupid!" cried Kiera, slapping the bars so hard her hand could have fractured.

She jumped back and cradled her painful hand, but her ire remained obvious.

"He threatened me, Sona, I'm so sorry!" Allira cried as she ran to the bars of Sonakshi's cage. "You have to believe me! He took my tail off with some type of magic and said I'd never get it back on unless I did what he said! And I really, really, needed my tail!"

"And what was it that he said you had to do?" asked Kiera furiously, running over to grip the bars dividing their cages.

"Just... just to spy on you and tell him what you were up to. I had to send a letter daily."

"I can't believe this," Kiera said, throwing herself down on the concrete floor. "This is my worst night-mare. For a friend to betray us..."

She looked downcast, shaded in abject misery.

Sonakshi just stared at Allira.

"You are not our friend," she said, her voice flat. "I could never trust you, ever again."

Allira stepped back from the cage, her head bowed low.

"Forget about them," said the man in the green

dress, coming forward. "I have a spare pigeon you can use to send this letter."

But Allira wasn't listening.

She lunged away from him and bounded out of the compound and into the bushes.

"Oi!" he shouted after her.

"Don't worry, Glen, she probably had something else to do."

Glen turned his one eye onto Sonakshi.

"Tomorrow, we go to market. Gary knows someone in a Columbian zoo that will pay a lot of money to have you, little horse."

Gary walked over to the wall and pressed a button.

A soft buzzing nose erupted from the bars around Sonakshi.

"And that, "Gary said. "Is to stop you from getting any ideas. One touch of the bars… and *zap!*"

Sonakshi's plan to use her bobby pin to pick the lock had just gone down the drain.

They had now electrified the bars of her cage.

The captors laughed, slapping each other on the back and walking away.

Sonakshi and Kiera gave each other a sad look.

"I can't believe they both abandoned us," grumbled Kiera.

"We did so much for them," Sonakshi sighed.

"We should have realised about Allira though. She knew where we were going without asking, remember? She said, "if you're going to the Bay…"

It didn't matter now. It was done, and Sonakshi felt sick to the stomach. She had been wrong to trust Allira, and she certainly wouldn't make that mistake again. Really, in her situation, she should not be trusting anybody. Now, she felt so sad, and tears welled in her eyes. She liked trusting… it made her feel normal, like everyone else. It made her forget about her fears of being hunted down, and chased, and captured—and, ultimately, killed.

The tears fell.

She could see the truth.

She was *not* normal, and never could be.

Her parents were right, and the world was a very dangerous place. And now their very fears were coming true. She was going to be sold off like a bird into a zoo. But that wasn't the worst of it. Rowen would then also be doomed.

"Mankini's boat leaves tomorrow," Kiera said in a low voice.

"We have to get out of here!" cried Sonakshi.

"Unless you have a way of getting rid of our electric bars…"

Kiera sighed and punched her fist into the ground.

Then she pressed her hands against her eyes and sobbed too, just like her friend.

Sonakshi wanted to cry, and cry, and cry some more. She wanted to break down these bars and go and save Rowen! She had never felt more alone than right now in this instant. And she was still bitterly angry with Kiera for getting them into this hellish mess. And she was angry with Allira and Miro for betraying them and leaving them on their own, captured, held hostage.

She stared glumly at the concrete wall in front of her.

* * *

The sky was still dark as night when Glen and Gary woke them up.

"Morning!" said Glen, still in his green dress. His voice sounded oddly vibrant, as if he was just giving a cheery good morning to a dear pair of friends.

The girls sat bolt upright at the same time, fear in their eyes.

"It's still nighttime!" protested Kiera thickly, sitting up.

"No sweet, it's three a.m. Time for my lions to feed."

Keys jangled, and Glen unlocked Kiera's cage.

"No!" cried Sonakshi, "Don't! Don't touch her!"

But Gary could not care less. He lurched into the cage and grabbed Kiera by the arm.

And then two things happened very quickly.

CHAPTER TWELVE

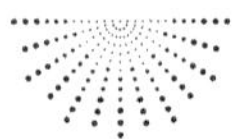

I saw him through the trunks of a field of coconut trees. It started as a moon-like glow in the darkness and solidified into the form of a large white-winged stallion with a brilliant horn that appeared to be made of a glittering crystal. The being emitted his own light and was so silent I was concerned that I was imagining the whole thing.

"Hello there," I whispered.

He threw his head and shook out his mane. Then he said something in a deep, melodic voice that I cannot repeat here, for it was too wondrous, too personal, too deep in nature that it would do the entire experience an absolute disservice to reveal.

—Lord Anthony Godfrey, *The Annals of Unicorn Sightings of the 16th Century, 1701.*

First, a commanding voice cried out behind them.

"Unhand her you traitorous peanut!"

And second, an arrow flew through the air and embedded itself deep in Glen's shoulder.

He cried out in shock and incensed rage.

Gary let go of Kiera and ran out of the cage.

"Stop!" he cried, running over to Glen, whose dress was now over his head. It was very lucky he was wearing his pants underneath!

And then, through the darkness, Sonakshi saw a group of people running towards them. Leading them all was a girl a little younger than herself. Sonakshi gasped in surprise.

The girl's skin was the colour of creamy milk chocolate and her eyes a dark forest green that were currently blazing with anger and authority. Her hair was a swirl of pastel purple and pink, her tiny, delicate braids topped with a small gold tiara.

More dazzling still were the gold and pink butterfly wings emerging from her shoulders. They flapped delicately as she ran towards them. Sonakshi instantly knew her to be a fairy.

A group of fairies with similar wings and hair followed her at a run; two of them had bows held at the ready. Another arrow flew and hit Gary in the foot.

He gasped in pain and fell to the ground where he stood.

"Sona!" cried a voice, "Kiera!"

To Sonakshi's further surprise, Miro came running up behind the girl with the pink hair.

"Miro!" Kiera and Sonakshi shouted. "I can't believe it!"

The colorful group reached the cages, panting.

"We went to find help," Miro said, coming up to Sonakshi's cage. "I hope you didn't think I'd left you. You'd saved me, so I couldn't do that."

"I wouldn't have put it past you to abandon us," said Kiera, cheerfully, but Sonakshi scowled at her rudeness. "But did you say 'we'?" Kiera went on.

Allira's brown face popped up from the back of the group.

"Yes, Allira is here too. If it weren't for her, I would've never found the fae."

Sonakshi and Kiera exchanged an uncertain look. Sonakshi chose to ignore Allira.

"I can't believe we got tricked," Sonakshi said, looking around at the fae now gathered in front of them. "It sure has taught me a lot about trusting… and who not to trust."

The lead fae picked up some keys off the ground and came to open Sonakshi's cage.

"You can trust us. And as for getting tricked, well, it happens," she said, pointing to the man in the green dress, whimpering in pain, clutching his injured shoulder. "Sometimes, things are not as they appear to be. The beautiful can be awful and the awful can be beautiful. Never judge a being by their appearance."

"This is very wise," said Sonakshi, walking out of her now open cage. "I will not be making that mistake again."

"Please," said Kiera, "Tell us who you are. You must be royalty!"

The fairy smiled at them.

"I am Vidya, the Princess of the Eastern Bushland Fae. I rule this part of the forest."

"Fae?" asked Kiera, looking at the beautiful girl in wonder.

"Yes, I am a fairy. Our kind do not frequent the busy parts of the world. We like to stay hidden in our Sky Palace. It was lucky Allira and Miro here found us and told us what had happened to you, so that we could come and help."

"Miro is brilliant," said Kiera fondly.

Miro fluffed his wings proudly.

All his grumpiness and scowling from earlier seemed to have melted away. Now, he was simply revelling in being hailed a hero. He puffed up his giant feathers again, peacock-like.

"We had heard of the fae palace," Miro said. "It was only by luck Allira caught up to me and we found one of the Guards gathering berries. We explained what had happened and who you were and they jumped in to help."

"You have keen eyes, Allira," said Vidya with a smile.

She then turned towards the men on the ground.

"Now!" she said in a commanding voice as two of her guards freed Sonakshi from her cage.

"Gary and Glen! I charge you with defying the Law of the Forest! I have now stripped of your land and we will imprison you for your crimes," cried Vidya.

The two men gasped in horror.

"N—No! Not our lands, Princess, please."

"Are you aware you have captured and threatened the Unicorn Princess and her Royal friends?" she asked in a harsh tone.

The men's mouth gaped open, looking from Sonakshi to Vidya in shock.

"There is no punishment big enough for that. You will rot in jail!" She now looked to the guards. "Tend to their wounds and take them from my sight!" she commanded.

The Guards carried the men away.

"I always knew they were up to something," said Princess Vidya. "I just had to catch them at it. We will have to treat the trees with magic so that eventually, they can be safe for travellers to eat again. They used to be such a source of replenishment, and they spoiled it all."

"You can do that?" asked Sonakshi curiously. "I mean, you can revert the trees?"

"Yes, fae magic works really well on plants. In the meantime, I will post some guards to protect the garden. And I must relocate those lions."

"Thank you for saving us," said Kiera.

"No problem at all," said Vidya, brightening. "You must be hungry and tired after this entire affair. It's late, so come along to my palace, and we'll get you some unpoisoned food."

Kiera flinched visibly at the use of the word poison. She felt the shadow of blame cast over her again as Sonakshi threw her a sideways, glowering look.

The two girls thanked Vidya profusely as she led

them out of the magical garden and down the road. Sonakshi was still furious at Kiera, so she walked as far away as possible from her, next to Princess Vidya. Kiera, in turn, cast Sonakshi a dark look and stuck next to Miro, chatting with him instead. And as for Allira—well, she simply trailed along behind them all, talking quietly with one of the fae. It was clear neither of the girls would ever fully trust her again, and so it was pointless to talk to them until they had completely accepted her.

Anyway, it looked like she'd got her wish to see the fae after all.

That kind of made up for all the stress of the past days.

But Sonakshi couldn't believe it. She mulled everything over.

Both Kiera and Allira had put them in such danger and didn't even think. Kiera, in fact, was *never* thinking and always doing. Sonakshi always planned and thought so carefully, and Kiera had to just come along and ruin everything in one fell swoop, with one stupid, rash action.

And Allira… well, she didn't even know what she thought about the kangaroo's betrayal. She was so angry; she didn't think she could ever talk to either of them again.

"Princess Vidya," murmured Sonakshi in as low a voice as she could muster. "Allira betrayed us. She is a servant of the evil witch Mankini. If your palace is supposed to be kept secret, we might be putting you in danger by bringing her. You should offload her."

Vidya considered Sonakshi's words for a moment.

"She was responsible for bringing us to you though. Does that not redeem her?"

Sonakshi shook her head. "She did save my life, yes. But she betrayed me after I helped her. And she lied horribly. And she may still be in contact with the witch. *I* cannot trust her."

Vidya nodded. "That's true, she could be. But I can see a great sadness in her, so she surely feels terrible. But as a precaution, I will blindfold her. That will safeguard us all."

Princess Vidya whispered to a fae next to her.

He headed off towards the end of their group, a strip of coloured cloth in his bag.

Sonakshi felt a little bad as Allira had told them it was her dream to meet the fae. Having them blindfold her seemed a little harsh, but she was in contact with Mankini. It felt right to hide some things from her, if not to send her on her way altogether.

They didn't walk far before Vidya led them off the path and into the bush. She explained that the Fae Palace was well hidden in the gumtrees so that no one could stumble upon it by accident. The Fae were private people and liked to stay separate from the rest of the world.

Vidya led them through a maze of trees until she found the one she was looking for. It was an enormous gum tree with a large trunk and branches that stretched out wide above them.

Vidya tapped at a particular spot on the base of the trunk and a small section of the tree glowed yellow.

When the light faded, a small door had appeared. Sonakshi and Kiera 'oohed' in wonder as Vidya gave them a smile over her shoulder before gently pulling the door open.

Inside, Sonakshi could see the beginnings of an entirely new forest.

They followed Vidya through the door.

Then, they gathered on the other side, looking around in wonder.

"Welcome to the Fae lands," said Vidya proudly. She held her arms wide, in a way of saying, *look at this. All this is for you to enjoy!*

It was a forest like no other.

Through the dark of night, everything glowed. The leaves of the trees shone a luminescent green, each flower emitting its own pastel light of oranges, yellows, pinks, and blues.

They walked through the forest in awe, trying to see everything at once.

Even Miro had nothing to say. His head seemed to spin around and around.

And the smell! The air itself smelled magical with an aroma of lavender and sticky cinnamon sweetness all at once. It made the travellers feel pleasantly dazed.

"The smell of the Concine trees is very nice," said Vidya. "But don't breathe in too much of it, it'll make you go loopy."

"This is nothing," said one of the fae guards. "Wait till you see the palace."

Allira had been led carefully through with her blindfold on, and now they took it off. Sonakshi looked away and into the forest, not wanting to make eye contact with her ex-friend, the one she absolutely did not trust anymore. But she still felt bad about the blindfold.

Allira gazed around, stunned as her black eyes readjusted to their freedom.

Something shimmered in the forest between the trees in the distance. Sonakshi took two steps towards it and it moved towards her too. Then she realised what it was and her breath got stuck in her throat. It was made of shimmering light, see-through and definitely not solid, with a long powerful body, a magnificent white mane and a long sparkling horn.

It was undoubtedly, a unicorn.

It pranced toward her and tossed its head, just once.

Then it turned away and faded into the dark of the trees.

"Oh no—" she whispered. She wanted to say, 'don't go! Or 'please stay!' but he was well and truly gone.

"Sonakshi?" Princess Vidya said, stepping softly behind her, "did you see something?"

Sonakshi shook her head, confused. Had it been real? It looked more like a ghost than anything. "No… no, I—I don't think I did."

"You saw nothing, then?" the fae asked gently.

"Nothing—like I said. I think so, anyway."

She didn't even know if there was supposed to be a right answer to that question.

And now she was confused, and untrusting—even of her own eyesight.

Vidya smiled. "The fae forest can show a person

many things, if they are willing." She laughed and shrugged. "It can also be very dangerous. We'd better go find the path."

They followed the others and stepped carefully through the forest for a few minutes until they came to a path paved with what looked like pure gold. It shone brightly and blindingly, reflecting the light of the trees and flowers around it.

When Sonakshi stepped onto it, she saw her own diamond horn reflected in it too.

"You could belong here," murmured Vidya in her ear. "You and your spectacular horn. But there, you can see the palace now."

And indeed, Allira, Kiera and Miro were standing on the path as if stuck in place.

The path ended abruptly at the edge of a cliff.

Sonakshi gasped and the fae guards around them laughed delicately.

The Fae palace was nothing like Sonakshi's castle.

Her palace was lovely enough, with its sturdy walls, tall turrets, and gleaming windows. But Princess Vidya's palace… it was something else.

Under a sky full of twinkling lights, the palace shone like its own star. It hung alone in thin air, supported by a thick golden cloud. It gleamed gold and silver, with curling spires that soared towards the sky and sparkling pillars leading to grand entrance doors.

But oddly, there did not seem to be any path leading towards or away from it.

"You must not have a thieving problem," said Miro dryly. "If no one can get to your home."

Princess Vidya laughed cheerfully.

"No indeed. Anyone that can't fly can't even get to it! So if we had a thief, the perpetrators would be easily identified."

She laughed again, more loudly this time.

As if on cue, a few of the winged guards stepped forward, fluttering so quickly it looked as though they didn't have wings at all. They were graceful, and everyone watched as they soared high across the empty starlight depths towards the castle.

Sonakshi's heart sank, and she turned her head to glance at her right wing.

It hung there, beautiful, and useless.

"None of us can fly," said Miro mournfully.

Princess Vidya looked at Sonakshi quizzically but didn't make a comment.

"Not to worry," she said cheerfully. "My forefathers already thought of that."

She stepped in front of the others, right on the edge of the cliff, held her the side of her hand to her mouth, and gave a high-pitched gurgling call.

It was both beautiful and strange, reminding Sonakshi of birds and clouds at the same time. Princess Vidya paused and gave the sound twice more.

From the distance, behind the palace, four pale shapes were soaring through the darkness towards them. The group waited patiently on the edge of the cliff and as the pale shapes came closer, Sonakshi realised that they were broad, fluffy clouds like cotton candy.

The four clouds came to a stop, lining one after the other along the cliff face.

Vidya stepped away from the edge, beaming at the group of visitors.

"Hop on then!"

Kiera was the first to go. She tentatively stepped to the edge of the cliff and placed a toe on the first cloud. It gleamed under the light of the full moon, a blue-grey colour.

"It's so spongy!" she exclaimed in surprise.

"Yes, it's very comfortable," said Vidya, laughing. "Please, take a seat."

Kiera put her other foot on the cloud and sat down carefully, peering down the side.

"Wow!" was all she could say.

Miro and Allira carefully got on their clouds, squatting down comfortably. Sonakshi was last and stepped onto hers, avoiding looking at the plunging dark depths below her. It surely would be a terrible end to an equally terrible few days if she plunged right off a cloud, to her death on the hard ground below. She chose to stand, and found it to be a stable surface.

"All righty, let's go!"

Vidya and her remaining guards ascended into the air, Vidya giving another bird-like call.

The clouds moved forward slowly, and the four friends clutched onto their clouds to steady themselves. The air was warm here, so they were very comfortable as the clouds flew them gently through the air towards the palace.

Sonakshi did not notice Vidya flying next to her until the Princess spoke.

"Your wings are lovely," she said. "They glow differently to mine."

"Yeah," said Sonakshi. "It's a shame I don't know how to use them."

"Oh?" said Vidya with interest. "They look strong, I'm sure you'll learn the technique. It took me years."

"Really?"

"Oh yes, with our wings, you have to flap them very fast. It takes time."

"Wow, I guess that's true; you do make them go fast."

"Yours won't have to do that though. You must move them strongly in a rhythm. It might also help if you do it from a height? Then you could just glide if you catch the right angle. That's what bats do, you know? They start off high, and plunge... We can try it off the cliff tomorrow if you like."

Bats. *Bats...* Sonakshi shivered at the very mention, but said nothing.

Sonakshi peered down at the inky, star-filled depths below. "But there doesn't look like there's anything below there."

"There isn't."

"Okay, then. No thanks."

The fae princess laughed.

Quickly, they arrived at the palace.

It looked even more beautiful up close, shining above them.

The four travellers stepped off their clouds onto the golden pathway. Vidya and the guards landed ahead of them, walking down the path, clearly happy to be home.

"Have you ever seen anything like this?" asked Miro, coming up next to Sonakshi.

"No way," she replied. "It's spectacular."

"I can't believe what luck you had finding them, Miro."

"Hm. Maybe not luck. Allira knew all the signs. It was really all her."

"Really?"

"Oh yes, I almost missed them amongst the bushes. They're very hard to see."

Sonakshi glanced at Allira. She was staring up at the palace, her mouth hanging open. Tears streamed down her eyes. Sonakshi's heart twinged. How could she have kept contact with Mankini even after knowing what had happened to Rowen?

But then again, Sonakshi remembered Allira's face when her tail had grown back. It really had meant everything to her. But Sonakshi did not make the same mistake twice.

Sonakshi *must not* make the same mistake twice.

She would not trust Allira. She *could* not. To trust could mean the death of her.

She had ignored her parents' stern warnings and careful protection of her, and in trusting the kangaroo, she had let them down and paid the price for it. Never again.

They reached the enormous front doors of the

palace, where two orange-winged fae stood guard with tall spears and shining gold helmets.

They let the group through an immaculate grand hall with a double staircase leading up to the next level. The guards dispersed to their own quarters.

Sonakshi turned back into her human form and Vidya smiled at her.

"I'll take you up to your guest rooms and have some food brought up for you," she said. "We can talk some more tomorrow, but I am sure you are exhausted."

Sonakshi and Kiera exchanged a look.

"Princess Vidya, in the morning, we are expected upon a ship in Freshwater Bay. We shouldn't stay too long."

Vidya's pink brows knitted together. "Ships do not usually anchor at Freshwater. Whose ship is it?"

Sonakshi hesitated. But these were the fae. Surely they would have advice for her.

"The witch Mankini has kidnapped Kiera's brother and has taken him to Fiji. In exchange for his life, I must give a drop of my blood. She is the one who is sending a ship for us."

"Then you cannot not take that ship."

"Pardon?"

"If this is Mankini of Makogai, you are in grave danger, Princess Sonakshi."

Vidya studied the look of fear and overwhelm in Sonakshi's speechless figure. "Come. We must talk in private."

CHAPTER THIRTEEN

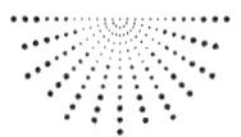

I saw a unicorn talking to himself in a low, cheerful voice. Then I realised he was not alone. The eternal companion of the unicorn is of a species more elusive than itself.
—Lord Andrew Godfrey, *The Annals of Unicorn Sightings of the 16th Century, 1701.*

Sonakshi gave Kiera an alarmed look and followed Vidya down a corridor, into an elegant room with wall-to-wall bookshelves.

"I do wish my father were here," Vidya said. "He is away at a conference, but he knows way more than I do about this."

Sonakshi's heart was beating fast.

She needed to get on that ship to get Rowen back. There was no other way.

Vidya untied the string that kept her quiver of

arrows tied to her back. She set it down and sat in a large red chair opposite a small fireplace.

"You need to sit too," she instructed.

Sonakshi reluctantly took the winged-back chair opposite her.

"What's this all about?"

"What do you know about Mankini?"

"She was after me as a child. And now she's dying, she needs a drop of my blood to live."

"You really think she only wants *one* drop of your blood?"

Sonakshi frowned.

Vidya rubbed her eyes tiredly.

"My father told me all about you. He was there that night when your parents fled Fiji."

Sonakshi's stomach tightened. The man with the blue beard.

"Does he have a blue beard?"

Vidya smiled. "You remember him? That's amazing."

"Vaguely. I was three."

"Your parents were fearful, so they tried to protect you by hiding the truth. But I would say that given your current predicament, the time for fear is over. Now I must protect you by *telling* you the truth.

"You know that you inherited your unicorn trait from your great-great-grandfather? But you must also know that unicorns are immortal. So, didn't you ever wonder how he was killed?"

Something stirred within Sonakshi. A dark shadow had fallen over Vidya's face.

She did not like where this was going.

"Unicorns are often killed for their blood. Drink some blood and you will gain exceptional health and maybe some temporary powers. Drink *all* their blood and you will gain their immortality. But then, the unicorn will die."

Sonakshi found it hard to breathe.

"One hundred and fifty years ago, Mankini killed your grandfather in Fiji. Yes, she became immortal, but she also had to pay the price. And so it disfigured both her and her magic."

Sonakshi stared out the window, her eyes prickling. Mankini had killed her grandfather. Something in her belly felt hot, and it trickled through her veins.

"But she already has my great-great grandfather's blood. Why does she want mine?"

"We believe that there is a book that has this information, a clue as to why she needs you. We have been trying to locate it with little success. We… also believe that your great-great grandfather wrote that book."

The heat in Sonakshi's veins flared.

Mankini killed my great-great grandfather.

The only person Sonakshi could have learned from. The only one who would have rendered her no longer alone, and the only one who would have understood her.

Her family. And he had been killed. For his blood.

"Sonakshi?"

Her attention brought her back to Vidya. "My guess is that she is going to try to reverse the curse of the unicorn while trying to keep her immortality. How she plans on doing that, I do not know. It would take a lifetime of searching to find the answer."

Sonakshi bristled as her anger rose within, batting away any tiredness from her restless night in the cage. Vidya must have seen this, and she stood.

"Here." She walked over to a bookshelf and slid out an old leather-bound book with yellowed pages. She handed it to Sonakshi, gently brushing off dust with her fingers.

"I think you should have this. I've read it before and books like this are scarce in your world. Here, take it. It's yours."

Sonakshi's anger cooled as she balanced the book on her lap like a delicate baby. It was titled in faded gold lettering:

The Annals of Unicorn Sightings of the 16th Century. Lord Andrew Godfrey.

"This is very precious, thank you."

She found it hard to speak through the lump in her throat.

"Make sure you read it on your voyage east."

Sonakshi looked up at her in confusion.

"I thought you said I shouldn't go on Mankini's ship."

"I'm... not telling you to go," she said slowly. "How could I? I also believe that if you do not go, your Rowen will die."

Sonakshi pressed her new book to her heart and gulped. That wasn't a choice at all.

"The choice is yours. But if you do decide to go, you should take one of my boats instead. They are faster and will give you an element of surprise. You stand more of a chance that way."

Sonakshi nodded. "Thank you, we will take you up on your offer. I cannot stand to be safe at Rowen's expense."

"Very well. It is almost dawn. Rest awhile and I will send for you."

"Thank you."

Vidya walked her back down through the corridor and through several passageways to the guestrooms, where she could hear Miro and Kiera chattering excitedly through the door.

"Thank you, Princess Vidya. This has been very difficult for us all."

The fae princess smiled warmly at her.

"There was a time when unicorns and fae were lifelong friends. Then the world became cruel, and those friendships became few and far between. I hope... we can be friends, Sonakshi, and start that alliance again."

Sonakshi's heart swelled and she felt soft tears stream down her face. She wiped her eyes with one hand and clutched her book with the other.

"Good friends are hard to come by. I'll take what I can get." And she remembered something someone said a long time ago, but she couldn't recall who it was. "Besides, I think me being a unicorn makes us cousins in a way."

* * *

Later that morning, the four of them awoke. Sonakshi had not spoken to Kiera or Allira the previous night, and they in turn had left her alone. She had a lot to think about, and she really wanted to read this book Vidya had given her. But time was pressing on them, and this recent information cast a weight on Sonakshi that wasn't sure she could share.

They ate quickly, before Vidya found them and took them back down to the forest.

She gave them a purple cotton bag.

"Take care of this one. This is your new food bag. As long as there is food in my palace kitchen, this bag will never fall empty."

Kiera took it with awe and Sonakshi had to bite her tongue before she said something rude. Luckily, Vidya averted their attention. "This is how the fae travel around the country. We cut back on a lot of travel with our portals. This one leads us straight into Freshwater Harbour.

They climbed through the eucalyptus portal and entered the brightly lit bay.

Sonakshi gasped in surprise. She had never seen such a thing.

Well, she must have when she was three, but she did not remember it. The blue ocean extended as far as the eye could see, glittering spectacularly under the blue sky.

A little way to her left was a long jetty, and an elongated yacht with bright purple sails sat patiently there.

"What a lovely boat," exclaimed Kiera to Vidya.

Vidya smiled and was about to walk them down to the jetty when Sonakshi halted them.

"Stop."

They looked at her quizzically.

"Allira, I'm sorry, but you can't come with us."

Allira's mouth opened and closed, then she nodded.

"I know you saved us yesterday, but I just can't trust you right now."

Sonakshi didn't know why she felt an enormous urge to cry right then and there, but she clenched her hands into fists and stopped herself from breaking down.

"I would like to say that I am truly sorry," said Allira in soft voice. "When that bat threatened me, I did not know you. But for the last few days, I had felt like we were becoming friends. And…" she held up her paw. "For the record, I saved your life twice. The first time was when I set the trap for the Yowie. He would have caught you otherwise. I care for you and Kiera." She bowed her head as if deeply hurt and upset.

Sonakshi nodded curtly.

Allira had a point. But was it enough?

Sonakshi couldn't help it.

One betrayal was too many and she could not get it out of her mind.

"You could have been honest with us," said Sonakshi. "Once you realised we were becoming friends, but you didn't. And all that time you were writing letters to Mankini…"

Allira hung her head even lower and stared at her paws. Miro and Kiera remained quiet.

"And that is why you shouldn't come with us. I am sorry, I still cannot trust you."

Sonakshi turned to Miro. He fluffed his feathers. "I know what you are going to say," he said. "But I would like to come with you if you will have me."

"Why?" Sonakshi needed to know what his reasoning was.

She could not handle being betrayed again—not by Miro either.

Miro took a deep breath.

"The last two days, being captured twice made me think about my life and what I've been doing with it. I don't want to waste away in this bushland… eating worms." He looked pointedly at Kiera, who gave him a small smile. "I want to do something with my life. And I think I can help you two. You need an older, more sensible creature to help you."

Kiera gave a very unladylike snort, and Sonakshi fought the urge to laugh.

She was still angry at Kiera, after all.

"Fine. Then we could use your help, Miro," said Sonakshi. "Thank you."

They gave Allira one last solemn glance and turned away, walking down the rocky plain onto the jetty where the yacht waited, *The Dancing Dimple* written across its side in gold.

CHAPTER FOURTEEN

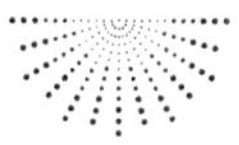

A unicorn's blood is power incarnate. Power can heal, power can love, power can control, power can destroy.
—Ma'afu Ma'ilei, *The Way of the Unicorn, 1863.*

Mankini sat in her rocking chair, a black beaded necklace in her hand, which she twisted fondly while staring at the boy with the red hair trapped there, behind the metal bars. She had built this cage for such a situation, and throughout her long life, had used it many a time, to house many an undeserving creature. Hay was scattered on the floor and two bowls sat in the corner. One was labelled "water", the other "food". On the other side sat a bucket, which her ever-loyal servant Batuman came and emptied once a day.

"Rowen," cooed Mankini. "You're such a pretty boy, aren't you?"

Rowen sat in his cell, with his legs hugged close to

his chest. He tucked his head into his knees and tried not to look at the haggard witch. His face and clothes made him look as though he had been dragged from his bed through the bush, dirt, and sea.

Which was, of course, exactly what had happened to him.

"All that red hair," Mankini continued mockingly. "I saw a unicorn in Ireland once, with hair like that. In his human form, of course. I caught just the briefest of glances before he disappeared. They are *rare.* That's where your family is from, isn't it?"

Rowen slowly lifted his dirty face from his knees and nodded his head.

"Hmm." Mankini scratched her chin and stared at him with her one functioning eye.

Batuman came along from the kitchen in the fortress's corner, clutching a small bowl in his hands. He waddled over to Rowen's cage and stopped in front of him.

"Bowl!" he commanded in his loud, croaky voice.

Rowen quickly grabbed the silver bowl labelled 'food' and brought it to the front of his cell, obedient as a pet dog, kneeling in front of Batuman as he always did. The old bat spooned a sloppy porridge-like mixture into Rowen's bowl. Rowen licked his lips as he watched Batuman intently. After the third spoon, Batuman turned away to walk back into the kitchen.

"Where is the next letter from the kangaroo, Batuman?" croaked Mankini.

Batuman turned to her and set the bowl down on the floor, clasping his claws behind his back.

"Ahem. Madam. There is no letter, I'm afraid. None today."

"Year after year," she droned on, unimpressed. "I am good to you, and time after time, you fail me, Batuman. Tell me why I should not use you as my next meal, hmm?"

Batuman let out a cry and threw himself at her feet.

"Batuman is working hard, Madam!" he sobbed. "Please, I know a letter will come soon. The last one told us—"

"That they were almost at Freshwater Bay. Yes, I know. But another letter came on the pigeon this morning."

She pulled a piece of paper from her sleeve and opened it, reading out loud.

"I am sorry to inform My Ladyship that the party you were expecting *did not board my ship today.*"

She rose from her seat like an erupting volcano, and threw the letter at Batuman. He straightened, turning the paper right side up on the floor for him to read with his own eyes.

"Please, Madam, they are but children; they are just running late is all..."

Mankini scoffed at him.

"Well, perhaps we should send them another letter?" She pointed a crooked finger at Rowen. "Perhaps we should send them a pretty ear as a memento?"

Rowen gasped and fled to the corner of his cell, whimpering and cowering.

"N-No! Please, I've done nothing wrong!"

Mankini thumped her fist against her chair, wincing in pain from the impact.

"I give the orders around here, Rowen, not *you*," she said nastily, "If I want to send them your ear, I will chop it off and send it."

She fidgeted in her chair. "I want something to spur them on is all."

She cast her eye about the room, thinking. Her gaze stopped at the wooden desk to her left, against the wall. She cocked her head.

"Where is the book, Batuman?"

"It was on your desk, Madam."

"It is not there!"

Her voice reached a crescendo, making the whole room shake and the pictures on the walls threatened to come crashing down with the immense vibrations.

Batuman wobbled over to the desk and climbed up the chair onto the desktop. Mankini bristled in her seat as Batuman walked along the length of the desk, his tiny claws gripping the edges, pushing papers here and there. "Uh, Madam—"

The chair creaked, and Batuman whirled around to see his mistress groan, leaning forward in her chair.

"No, Madam!"

Mankini growled, cussing under her breath, speaking words that made Rowen place his hands over his ears. She leaned forward, and with a gigantic creak of her bones, was up and out of her chair.

Batuman gasped, as—hunched, and arms swinging wildly—she shuffled to the desk to see for herself. She wheezed, staring at the table, hands outstretched.

"It's not here," she whispered, confused.

"Madam—"

"Someone has taken my book!" she yelled, her gnarled hand thumping down on the desk.

"It must be here, Madam. We just need to look a little closer. Maybe you moved it... you know, to someplace safe, Madam." He trembled, his little bat ears and whiskers quivering.

"I did not move it, Batuman! I *did not move it,* you hear me?"

Batuman cast his eyes about the fortress, searching for any clue, any answer to account for the strangely missing volume. Wherever could it have gone?

Mankini growled in anger, her face deep red and purple now, and she turned, whipping around and looking at every angle, surface, and orifice of the room for the first time in weeks.

Fury rose up within her, burning hot and heavy. This was not supposed to happen. This was impossible! No one was allowed to read that book. She had won it fairly. It was hers, forever!

She snatched Batuman from the desk and shuffled to the window, holding him uncomfortably tight. He squirmed but she only squeezed harder, moving her stiff arm backwards and then sharply hurling him straight out the open window. It was a horrible shock for Batuman, but also a relief to be let go. He had been sure she would throttle him.

"Find my book!" she screamed with malice. "You hopeless, useless creature! Find it!"

She watched him flap his wings frantically and then

right himself, taking flight towards Fiji. Panting, Mankini watched as the black blob of Batuman grew ever smaller. She panted at the window and an itsy, bitsy, teeny trickle of fear entered her usually impenetrable heart.

CHAPTER FIFTEEN

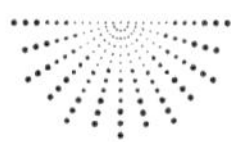

Unicorns have flown since time began. Listen to the wind. Listen to the sky. But most of all, listen to yourself, for that pulls you higher than any other thing in this world.
—Ma'afu Ma'ilei, *The Way of the Unicorn, 1863.*

"Urgh!"

Kiera leant over the rail of the boat, hurling the contents of her belly into the sea.

Having lived inland all her life, she hadn't known she would be seasick; she had never been on a boat before. But they had been at sea for the past twelve hours now.

Vidya had shown them how to use *The Dancing Dimple,* and they had left swiftly. And for that entire time, Kiera had fought her own battle with seasickness.

"I told you not to drink all that strawberry milk," said Miro unhelpfully from as far away as he could get from her.

Kiera straightened and turned to face him, her face an unhealthy shade of green.

"I think I'll go lie down," she said, feebly.

Clutching her belly, she ambled towards the stairs, lurching this way and that with the rocking of the vessel, her legs reacting like those of an uncertain newborn deer.

Down a set of creaky stairs and under the boat, Princess Vidya had tied up three comfortable purple hammocks, each of which swung in time to the motion of the deep sea.

Sonakshi's anger at Kiera had decreased when she realised that without their brief capture, they would never have been found by Princess Vidya, which actually had made their trip shorter. And now food was not an issue either. Bearing all of this in mind, they had no reason to argue. But their relationship was still frosty, and they spoke to each other in short, curt sentences. It had metamorphosed into one of those awkward friendships that would never cut ties, yet had been damaged in a manner neither ventured to talk about. The issues were in the past now, but the frost between them refused to melt. And so, the girls sat in a strained silence, giving equally strained and occasional smiles. Neither knew how to behave now.

Miro went to Sonakshi, sitting in human form on an elevated platform at the helm of the boat, where the large circular steering wheel was housed. He surveyed the things she had laid out on a table before her. Sonakshi had found these stowed inside the desk next to the helm.

There were maps of the Pacific Ocean, one of Fiji, and another of Makogai.

Next to these were silver instruments he guessed were for navigating the seas.

"I never asked you, Princess, do you know how to sail?" he asked, coming to sit beside her.

"No," Sonakshi said, shrugging, "But Princess Vidya said they enchanted this ship, so it'll go where we tell it to with no trouble. I shouldn't even have to touch the controls."

Miro nodded, but worry was still spread across his face.

"How will you get one million gold pieces?" he asked.

"You're kidding, right? I won't be giving that witch a single thing," said Sonakshi angrily. "We have to show her that she can't mess with us."

"You're very brave, then, Sona," said Miro. "I'm not sure I could stand up to her."

"I just don't like bullies."

"What do you think will happen when we get to Makogai?"

"I don't know," she said honestly. "I think we still have a way to go before I even think about that." She looked out at the wide blue ocean in front of them, where the waves went endlessly on. She took in a deep breath. "It's a lot of water, isn't it?" she breathed.

Miro nodded in agreement.

"Big enough to hide a lot of things. I've heard all sorts of things exist in the deep. Underwater cities where merpeople live, fishes that grow lights from their heads so they can see in the dark, plants that glow… all sorts of strange and wonderful things."

"There's so much to learn out here in the real world. I can't believe what's happened in such a short time. Not so long ago, I was cocooned in a make-believe world, so I see now."

Miro nodded.

"Yes, well, that Yowie, and the fae… I guess I'm just a magnet for danger."

Sonakshi laughed. "At least we can say that we saved each other."

Miro laughed and fluffed his wings.

"After all this is over, you should come and see my palace. It's nothing like the fae one, of course…"

"Oh, that would be lovely. Do you have books there?"

"Plenty, we have an entire library," Sonakshi answered, beaming, thinking of the books.

Miro whistled through his beak.

"I do love to read; I've even learned to turn the pages with my beak," he said, dreamily.

"You're very skilled at many things, Miro! Thanks for coming with us," offered Sonakshi.

"Well, it seemed a lot more interesting than going back home," Miro said.

Sonakshi laughed. "*Interesting* is one word for it."

Miro hesitated, opening his beak once, then closing it.

He took a deep breath, "Princess Vidya told you something important, didn't she?"

"How did you guess?" she asked darkly.

"Kiera said she was worried about it."

"She could've told me that."

"Could she?"

Sonakshi sighed, it was true; she had not been very kind to Kiera of late. The truth of it was, her emotions swayed and rocked in her, just like they were rocking in the sea right now.

She felt heavy with knowledge. She felt angry. And she was tired.

Mankini had to pay for what she had done to her great-great grandfather. She had to pay for what Sonakshi had lost. Her blood fizzed and boiled and her own emotions scared her. She was on foreign land on the inside as well as the outside. Most of all, she did not feel like sharing that. *She* was the unicorn princess; it was hers to bear alone. Kiera or Miro couldn't help her.

But she was glad they were here with her all the same.

And so they continued on the next day, sailing through the Pacific Ocean. They swung on her hammocks and Miro gave them riddles, telling them all about his family.

"I'm the cleverest in my family," Miro proclaimed, that afternoon, "but my sister, now, she is an artist. Brilliant with a paintbrush, I tell you."

"How does she paint though?" asked Kiera, confused.

"With her beak," he said, casually, "with a brush

made of human hair. Willingly given, of course," he added quickly, upon seeing their horrified looks.

They ate the limitless food Princess Vidya had given them, even able to do a bit of cooking in the tiny oven next to their hammocks, enabling an awkward Kiera—sadly not blessed with culinary abilities—to bake an undercooked vegetable pot pie and sunken lemon cakes.

The weather was pleasant, cloudless, with a warm, beaming sun and swift wind that made their yacht fly through the ocean, ruffling Miro's feathers rudely.

That night, Miro told them ghost stories. Sonakshi and Kiera huddled together under their own blankets, close to the warm stove, and Miro sat opposite them, making shadow puppets with his wings and feet. He had an excellent collection of stories, some scarier than others, because he was the eldest of many brothers and sisters.

Telling stories had been the only way to keep them quiet.

The next morning, Miro lifted his keen nose to the air and sniffed. And the salty stillness in the air gave him shivers, being the type of stillness that came before something.

It felt as though the ocean was holding its breath, bracing itself.

Miro looked at their tiny yacht in the middle of the expanse of the ocean and his stomach did a little flip. Something was coming, and whatever it was, it was big.

But he put his head down and said nothing.

Sure enough, that afternoon, everything changed.

The storm hit them suddenly, head on.

Sheets of icy rain belted down and the clap of thunder made them jump where they sat in their cabin, their hammocks swinging violently from side to side.

A blast of wind tumbled through, making the yacht sway dangerously in the water. No amount of fae magic could hope to keep them still in his hurricane.

"It's right on top of us!" cried Miro. "Stay where you are!"

"I'm gonna be sick!" cried Kiera, scrambling out of her hammock and up the stairs.

"Where are you going?" called Sonakshi.

"She can't go up there!" yelled Miro over the sound of the thundering rain.

Sonakshi watched her with dismay. She knew Kiera could not go up to the deck alone. It was way too dangerous. With this wind and the way the yacht was swaying, she could easily get pulled off the boat and into the ocean. And with waves like this, magical yacht or no, there would be no way of getting her back. "Kiera! No, you'll end up overboard!"

Sonakshi leapt off her hammock and transformed into her unicorn self, galloping up the stairs. Miro's yells followed her as she reached the darkness of the deck. Rain pelted down on her like bullets, and lightning flashed across the sky, revealing black clouds hovering above them. The sea rolled dangerously underneath, making the yacht lurch and sway like a rollercoaster. Up and down they went, making walking across the deck to Kiera almost impossible. She was bent over the rail at the end of the yacht, still hurling her guts up.

Sonakshi was halfway to her, squinting to see through the heavy rain.

"Kiera!" she called, "You're too close to the edge! Kiera!"

A large swelling wave crashed into the yacht and the whole thing lurched sideways.

Kiera toppled over with a scream, sliding all the way to the other side of the yacht, and hitting the railing hard. Sonakshi, too, lost her footing and scrambled to get back onto her hooves. Behind her, she heard a shout and Miro leapt onto the deck.

"Get back down!" Sonakshi said, "it's too dangerous!"

"We can help!" cried Miro, and being much lighter on his feet, he quickly overtook Sonakshi and reached Kiera crumpled against the railing, arm held up against the rain.

Sonakshi got to her feet as the yacht swayed again. Miro reached his long neck down and Kiera used him to help her stand up, one hand over her mouth.

"Let's get back down!"

They turned as a group towards the staircase, just as the rain ceased pelting down, then stopped completely. The air cleared and they could see across the ocean.

And then they saw *it.*

And their hearts turned to ice.

Out of the sea, an impossibly gigantic tentacle, at least twice as large as the biggest tree trunk, rose into the air. The group froze in their tracks, staring at it in shock.

The grey-green tentacle advanced towards them, feeling its path through the air, twisting this way and that. Their eyes widened as they saw it up close now, large suckers lining the base.

The tentacle reached as high as the mast of the yacht and, with its tip, it felt along the top of the mast and sail. The little boat shook slightly, and the tentacle moved down the mast, as if seeing the dimensions of their boat and inspecting what it was made out of.

The group stood so still, holding their collective breaths, as the tentacle reached the base of the mast. It moved to the side of the yacht, running around the rails.

And as quickly as it came, it left, snaking back into the water.

Sonakshi let out a sigh a relief… and then immediately choked.

Where the tentacle had disappeared into the ocean, in its place, an enormous piercing blue eye set in a slimy grey-green, oval-shaped head hovered over the surface of the water. It looked at Sonakshi, Miro, and Kiera, one by one.

Its pupil grew bigger, its black depth striking fear into Sonakshi's heart.

It dipped back below the water. Sonakshi had seen

pictures of gigantic octopus-like creatures as big as her castle in books before.

"Kraken!" Miro screamed.

He swung into action, pushing Kiera in the back and making her stumble towards the stairwell. Sonakshi followed close behind.

Their efforts were in vain, however, because almost immediately, *two* huge tentacles shot into the air towards the boat, grabbing it on either side, and heaving it this way and that.

Miro and Kiera screamed in terror.

The Kraken snapped the front of the boat clean from its hull.

"The boat! The boat! It's taken it right off!" said Kiera.

"We're going to capsize!" Miro cried.

"Nooooooo! Stop it! Stop it!" Kiera shrieked, clutching her face in horror. She pushed Miro aside and ran to the rail.

"Stooooop!" she shouted into the water.

But the kraken must not have liked this because a humongous tentacle now shot towards her, grabbed her tightly around the waist, and pulled her high into the air.

She screamed, and Miro and Sonakshi watched in horror.

Kiera's arms and legs flailed and she screamed, a horrifying sight to behold.

The giant tentacle leaned back in the air and then launched forward, lurching, tossing the helpless and terrified girl right over the top of the boat and into the rolling sea on the other side.

Sonakshi screamed and ran to the rail, watching Kiera's body plummet into the waves far away, water splashing high. She did not come back up to the surface.

She was gone; the hungry ocean had swallowed her up.

It pelted down with rain again, accompanied by the sound of riotous, distant thunder.

Miro wailed with despair, in time to the rumble of the storm.

They watched the kraken's great tentacle slipping back underneath the water, not to be seen again. The water rippled just a little on its surface and became still, as if the kraken had never been there. It seemed it had only come to do a job, and now it was done, the kraken was satisfied to return to wherever it had been hiding, down in the murky depths. Sonakshi did not think.

She did not let the fear rising within her take over, and just knew she had to act.

In desperation, she took a run up, and galloped to the edge of the yacht, jumping into the air as she'd practiced days ago.

She flapped her wings hard, rising into the air, but the wind and rain battled against her. Over the surface of the grey water, she beat her wings harder, but the wind's onslaught was too strong. She lost her height and a sudden gust sent her shooting down into the icy water.

Enormous waves rolled and crashed alongside her.

"Sona!" Miro shouted from what seemed like very far away.

Oh no, she thought, as a tremendous wave rose up, crashed on top of her and sent her, like a toy, into the depths of the ocean.

CHAPTER SIXTEEN

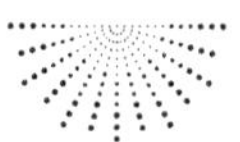

It takes great skill and courage to use a weapon as a tool for good. Such is a unicorn's horn. It is wielded with utmost respect and sincerity. To be touched by a unicorn's diamond horn is an honor attained with more difficulty than knighthood.
—Ma'afu Ma'ilei, *The Way of the Unicorn, 1863.*

Sonakshi was floating in the ocean's cold embrace. She turned this way and that, searching the ocean for any sign of danger. But there was nothing, no kraken, just darkness.

She looked up. She was so far from the surface, and it was then she realised she was still floating downwards.

My hooves!

Her steel hooves and her heavy unicorn body were dragging her down!

She turned into her human form and tried to swim towards the surface; she kicked her legs and moved her arms, but grew tired quickly, and the surface did not move any closer to her.

There wasn't any way she could see to get out of this.

Her lungs were burning in her human form since they did not hold as much air.

She turned back to her unicorn self and felt herself sinking deeper into the depths. She moved her four legs, but it only made her sink yet more.

There was nothing she could do.

She felt dizzy and cold, and hopeless.

How could things have gone so wrong so quickly? They had fought their way here, only to be stopped in their tracks by a stupid underwater kraken.

And again, said a mean voice in the back of her mind. *You couldn't fly. You failed Kiera, and now she's gone. We're all gone.*

I wonder what they'll say about us, she thought numbly.

Then she thought about her mother. Would she really never see her parents again?

She closed her eyes and saw their faces, saw their pain and their longing to see her return.

The muted sound of thunder rumbled above her.

And within it, she almost thought she could hear her mother's voice, calling her.

She felt so tired, exhausted, and cold. She could definitely go for a nap about now.

She had not felt so exhausted since she'd eaten the

drugged pastries. It was a strange feeling of being so tired that nothing even seemed to matter anymore. She allowed her eyes to close.

* * *

Sonakshi was jolted awake. A harsh light shone through her eyelids, and she opened her eyes in fear. Was it the kraken?

It wasn't. The flickering shape of a unicorn hovered in front of her, beautiful and strong, the same ghost she had encountered before, from the fae forest.

How had it shown up here? The ghost unicorn tossed his head and seemed to smile at her. He floated closer, and Sonakshi heard a soft voice all around her.

Do not sail straight into Makogai; go to Suva first. The book you seek is there. Don't give up, my sweet...

Strong hands gripped her about her face, and the ghost was gone.

Sonakshi turned her head, shocked to be staring into the beautiful purple eyes of a girl.

The girl let her go, and Sonakshi saw that she wasn't really a girl at all.

In place of legs, she had a beautiful and glittering scaled fish's tail.

Sonakshi was being pushed from below, and now she saw two young mermen, with vibrant green tails and grinning pale faces, pushing her upwards.

The mermaid swam alongside her, and Sonakshi noticed she had a sword in her hand. She scanned the water left and right, searching for signs of trouble.

Sonakshi was moving upwards incredibly fast, the mermen swishing their tails strongly through the water, until finally…

"Ah!" Sonakshi gasped in the night air, the mermen still supporting her from below.

Sonakshi turned back into her human form and the mermaid grinned in surprise.

"Surprises for both of us!" Her voice was sweet but husky, as if she did not use it much. "Hello!" she continued. "We need to get you back to the boat. Your friend is already there."

Sonakshi's heart leapt. They had saved Kiera as well?

The merpeople rolled her onto her back and tugged her gently through the water as she deeply breathed the fresh ocean air. Her lungs burned, but she couldn't care less.

It had stopped raining, and she could see a bright white full moon hanging in a sky clear of the heavy rain clouds from before.

Sonakshi felt the merpeople slow to a stop, and she saw the mast of her yacht. She turned around and saw the narrow, worried face of Miro leaning over the rail.

"Oh Sona!" he squawked. "I can't believe it! I thought you were a goner for sure!"

The merpeople hauled Sonakshi onto the deck of the yacht, and she flopped down on a blanket someone had laid down.

The mermaid who had spoken jumped up to sit on the side of the boat to sit close by her, a glittering tail hanging over the side, and Sonakshi could see her clearly for the first time.

Her skin was the colour of milky tea, and her long black hair tumbled in beautiful wet waves down her back. On the top of her head was a tiara of shimmering coral and sapphire.

She wore a crop top of delicate shells coated in mother of pearl. Combing through her hair with her fingers, she watching Sonakshi curiously. A silver sword lay at her side.

"Thank you," said Sonakshi gratefully, "I thought—"

The girl waved her hand, "No worries. We had been following the kraken for the last few days. Needless to say, he has been causing trouble. You need not worry about him anymore, though. We're locking him up tonight."

Sonakshi could not imagine a cage big enough to hold that thing.

With a start, she realised she had not seen Kiera on the yacht. She whirled around and saw merpeople were repairing their yacht on the broken side on her left, and on her right, Miro was coming towards her with another blanket in his beak.

"Where is Kiera?" she asked, panicking.

He dropped the blanket around her shoulders and she tried to dry herself off.

"She is downstairs and not feeling so well. She coughed up a lot of water, but is okay otherwise."

"We got to her just in time," the mermaid said.

Sonakshi turned to look at her. She was so beautiful under the light of the moon.

"My name is Sonakshi, the Unicorn Princess of Macuata." She offered her hand.

The girl took her hand and shook it. "I am Meera, Mermaid Warrior Princess of the East Pacific Ocean."

"I like your sword."

"I like your wings."

Sonakshi sighed. "Well, I wish I could use them better."

"I saw your horn through the darkness," said Princess Meera. "You can use that pretty well."

Sonakshi smiled, grateful for her horn.

"Are they looking at our boat?" she asked, watching two mermen sitting on the side of the yacht, holding a broken-off piece. "I'm not sure how we're going to get to Makogai now."

"You're going to Makogai Island?"

"There is a hostage situation there with Kiera's little brother. I'm going to release him."

"Really? Well, we are very good at fixing boats. We'll have you on your way soon."

"You can do that?"

"Oh, yes, we help sailors all the time. Usually they don't know it, though. When I saw you were a unicorn, I knew we could show ourselves to you."

"I can't say thank you enough."

Meera smiled at her.

"You helped us too. The Kraken was moving so fast in the water I wasn't sure if we could catch up. But he stopped to attack your boat, giving us time to gain on him."

"Ah, well, glad we could be of service," said Sonakshi, laughing nervously.

Meera laughed back and then frowned over Sonakshi's shoulder.

"Stowaway!" came a cry.

Sonakshi and Miro turned to see merpeople pushing up a soaking mound of brown fur. A narrow head poked out, choking and spluttering.

"Allira?" said Sonakshi incredulously, rising to her feet.

Allira coughed up water and rubbed her bedraggled face. Sonakshi and Miro ran over to her. "Oh my God, Allira, how did you get here?"

"She was hiding in the hull of your yacht," came the deep voice of a merman in the water. "Once the water went in… she's very lucky."

Sonakshi couldn't do anything except pull Allira into an embrace.

She began to cry and Allira cried too.

"I… I'm so sorry, Princess, you have to believe me. I didn't mean to cause harm. I'm not in league with Mankini! Please believe me!" she sobbed. "I just wanted to come with you."

Sonakshi put two fingers under Allira's chin and tilted her face towards hers. She looked deep into Allira's wet black eyes and saw only honest, desperate sincerity.

"Oh Allira," Sonakshi embraced her again. "I forgive you. I can't believe you hid in our boat! That was such a stupid, dangerous…and sweet thing to do."

"I'm sorry, I'm sorry" she blubbered. "I couldn't bear to have you angry at me. I just wanted to help."

Sonakshi sighed, "Let's go underneath, hey? See if Kiera's okay."

Miro and Sonakshi helped Allira up and began walking towards the cabin.

"Do you have any food down there?" came Meera's voice. "I'm famished!"

"Oh!" said Sonakshi. "Please eat with us. We can make yummy food up in a jiffy."

"That is so very kind of you!"

Miro hurried downstairs to get Vidya's food bag, and Sonakshi helped Allira down the stairs, rubbing at her friend's soaked and scruffy fur with a fluffy towel.

When Kiera saw them, she tiredly lifted her head from her hammock.

"Sona," she said weakly.

"Oh Kiera, I was so worried." Sonakshi settled Allira into her own hammock and came over to Kiera to give her a hug. Kiera patted her on the back.

"I can't believe the merpeople saved us!" Kiera said.

Sonakshi fell on top of Kiera and felt hot tears fall down her cheeks. "I'm so sorry," she sobbed, "I can't believe I said all those things to you back at Emily's Garden. And I'm sorry for being mean and cold. Please forgive me. I should never have said—"

"No, it's true!" interjected Kiera. "I do eat a lot. I just shovel it all in..."

They both burst into laughter and Sonakshi righted herself. "Emily's garden wasn't your fault," said

Sonakshi. "We all missed the signs. Oh look! I'm sorry I cried all over you."

Kiera laughed. "Oof! I think I swallowed a tear of yours! That's okay. Unicorn tears never hurt anyone." Then she grimaced. "But... do you think it would be worth a try to use your horn to help me? I think I swallowed a lot of water down there... I don't feel so good."

Sonakshi wondered why she hadn't thought of it before. Her horn had healed Allira so spectacularly after all.

Why not try it to help Kiera?

Sonakshi flashed into her unicorn form and carefully lowered her head towards Kiera.

"Be careful!" laughed Kiera. "You don't want to kill me by accident. At least, I don't think you do, but judging by those looks you gave me earlier..."

Sonakshi gently and playfully nudged her with her elbow. "Hey, stop that!" she teased. "I wasn't that bad. My looks wouldn't have killed you."

"No, I know that," said Kiera softly. "Can we try your horn, then, please?"

She looked sad and sickly, her skin white and sweaty. Sonakshi really hoped this would work.

"Why don't you hold my horn?" asked Sonakshi, her head angled so she was facing the floor. "I can't see you from this angle, so just tell me when it's close. Please be careful."

Kiera guided Sonakshi's horn towards her chest and inhaled sharply. Sonakshi jumped back, thinking she had hurt her friend. But she hadn't. Instead of a wound, a bright yellow light had formed all the way around Kiera. It disappeared quickly.

Kiera sat up and put a hand over her chest.

"Oh wow, Sona! I feel a lot better!"

Sonakshi sighed in relief.

"Best friends?" asked Kiera.

Sonakshi nodded, "Always. And... I'm so sorry for before."

She looked ashamed and upset.

Kiera rested her hand on Sonakshi's own, and said, "Hey, it's over now. We were both silly."

Then she got off her hammock and helped Sonakshi do the same thing with Allira, who jumped up immediately with glee, flinging her arms around her friends.

After that, they all had enough energy to join Miro on deck with Meera, who was munching happily on a blueberry muffin. Sonakshi remembered that accepting food from strangers had led them astray in the forest. But Meera and the other mer people seemed quite happy to accept their food. They had saved the lives if Kiera and herself, there was a bond between them now. Invisible but strong.

Under the stars of the now clear night sky, the merpeople wolfed down the cakes and fresh tea, murmuring their thanks, and then returned to work on the boat.

They had their own type of magic, it seemed, because, as Sonakshi watched them off the side of the boat, they seemed to glue the boat together out of parts they pulled out of nowhere.

Shaking her head, Sonakshi wondered if anyone back home would believe them.

It didn't really matter though; she was just thrilled they were all alive.

The merpeople worked right through the night, hammering and screwing pieces of metal together with tools made of coral and shell. Some of them sat on the side of the yacht, and others worked, treading water in the ocean. The air grew hot and sticky after the storm had left, reminding Sonakshi of summer nights back at her castle.

They were heading into the tropical lands, where it was always summer, hardly ever winter.

"You've blown off course a little," said Meera cheerfully, "But with this boat fixed, you'll be back on course in no time."

They ended up laying their blankets down on the deck and fell asleep, looking up at the stars. Meera sang as her people worked, a slow merry song that sounded like lazy waves falling upon a moonlit beach. It felt to Sona, as if this were all a dream. Perhaps when she awoke in the morning, there had never been kraken at all.

But of course, in the morning, they woke up to an intact boat with Meera and the others still very much real.

"Wow!" said Miro, "It looks exactly like it did before the attack!"

The merpeople smiled and flicked their tails happily from the water.

As they shared breakfast, Sonakshi took her maps

to the side of the boat where Meera sat, and they whispered together, going over everything that Sonakshi would need to know about Fiji and Makogai. As a Princess of the Ocean, Meera was very knowledgable about the islands nearby.

After they all finished eating their fruit, they prepared to say goodbye to the merpeople.

"I know witches," said Meera, "they are tricky and clever people."

She handed Sonakshi a long sword with a hilt made of pink shiny coral inlaid with sapphires. The blade glittered in the sun.

"What is this?" asked Sonakshi, in awe.

"This is my shell-sword," said Meera. "This is my gift to you for your quest. She is called *Truth Seeker,* for she cuts through lies."

Sonakshi weighed the heavy sword.

She had seen nothing like it—beautiful and deadly at the same time.

Meera turned to the rest of the group, "For the rest of you, I give you these—"

She held out her palm in which four tiny conch shells lay.

"These are communication earpieces. My team uses them to talk to each other over long distances. Just put them in your ear and you'll be able to keep contact if you lose each other."

They each took one shell each and stared at them in wonder.

"This is marvellous technology," said Miro, tapping a shell Kiera held out for him to inspect.

"The wind is in your favour today," said Meera, her finger in the air. "You should reach Fiji by this afternoon."

"Thank you for all your help," said Kiera, "we will never forget you."

Meera and the merpeople splashed back in the water, gave them a wave, and swam away.

Sonakshi stood by the helm of the yacht and instructed the ship to set sail again.

"To Suva Wharf please," she said, and immediately, the wheel swung itself, wind filled the purple sails and the *Dancing Dimple* was off into the East.

Sonakshi gathered the others around her desk and took out the maps she had been studying.

"The capital of Fiji is called Suva," she explained, pointing to a map of Fiji. She indicated a point on the bottom side of Fiji.

"It is on the south-west side of Fiji. Once we get there, we'll set sail north-east to here—"

She pointed upward and to the right of the map where *Makogai* was written next to a tiny green island.

"Once we arrive in Suva, we'll—"

"Hold on," asked Kiera. "Shouldn't we be sailing straight to Makogai? We can't waste time going to Suva."

Sonakshi inhaled deeply. It was time to tell her friends the truth.

Or part of it, anyway.

She couldn't tell them about her ghost unicorn speaking to her; they'd think her mad. But she told them what Princess Vidya had told them, about how

Mankini was the one to have killed her great-great grandfather, and how they were not sure why Mankini needed Sonakshi's blood now. "… and so, the book that has this information is at Suva. We need to find it first."

"Are you sure?" asked Kiera, uncertain.

"I don't want to delay getting to Rowen any more than you do. But we have to go in there prepared. And my heart tells me to go to Suva, as clearly as it told me Allira isn't lying to us. We *need* to go there first, I know it."

Kiera nodded, her eyes blazing. "We're almost there."

Sonakshi nodded. "We're going to save him, Kiera. We will."

As they sailed that day, Sonakshi read the book Princess Vidya had given her and it lifted her heart. But at the same time, she could not but help feel a sense of foreboding. She was sure she had seen this ghost-unicorn twice now, but where had it come from? Now it was giving her directions, and in her heart, it felt right. This book, written by the very hand of her great-great grandfather, was somewhere in Fiji. This was the first time she would hear the words of another unicorn. But would it really have the answers she needed?

The answer to why Mankini needed her so badly?

And if she got the answer to that question, what would she be able to do with it? Would it be enough to save Rowen? And even if they saved Rowen, would Mankini still be after her?

She held the *Annals of Unicorn Sightings* book close

to her heart. All these unicorns out there... they sounded so wondrous and brave. *They* would surely have it in them to take a daring quest. But she was just ten, and not a *real unicorn* yet. Sure, she could use her horn.

But she had miserably failed to fly yet again, and that was that.

She was still a failure. What if she failed Rowen too? What if she never left Makogai?

As the late afternoon sun created deep orange streaks in the sky, Miro's emu-eyes were the first to notice something different on the horizon. "Land ho!" he called.

Kiera jumped up from her spot, sunbathing on the deck.

She peered into the distance, shielding her eyes from the light.

"Is that—"

"Fiji!" Sonakshi called.

A seagull soared above them.

"Finally!" said Kiera.

"We're not stopping yet, Kiera," said Sonakshi. "That must be Sigatoka. We have to travel around the coast to get to Suva Wharf."

"That's okay!" she replied, "I'm just happy to see greenery again!"

They could definitely see dense tropical greenery all around the island, and as they got closer, a tall mountain range too. The air was warm and humid, and it smelt like summer.

They reached Suva Wharf in the middle of the

night. Navigating between the other ships and yachts in the harbour, the *Dancing Dimple* found itself a safe spot to dock.

They chatted nervously.

"Oh, I'm so ready to be on land!" said Kiera, "Let's find this book quick smart!"

"It's very late," said Miro seriously, "we can't go running around in the middle of the night on a strange island. We should find a place to sleep on land and find it in the morning."

"There'll surely be a motel or an inn we can stay at," Sonakshi agreed.

"We can't waste time!" retorted Kiera. "Rowen could be in danger!"

"It's well past midnight, Kiera," replied Miro. "No one is that alert right now, we need to rest."

Kiera grumbled in her usual style, but agreed all the same.

"But wait!" said Miro, suddenly jumpy. "Allira and I can't go waltzing Matilda into Fiji. People will ask why a kangaroo and an emu are hanging around there. It's not exactly something they see every day."

"You're right, Miro," said Sonakshi. "We need to keep a low profile."

And so they dug through the contents of their bags and found suitable clothes as a disguise.

They covered Allira's ears with a brown cap and put a long dress on her.

For Miro, they put a shirt and pants on him and zipped him up in a long, casual jacket, stuffing the sleeves and top with material to make him look more like the shape of a man, trying to conceal his rotund torso balanced on stick-like, skinny legs.

Then they tied the pants tightly around his waist with a belt, stuffing yet more material down his legs. In the end, he looked like a rather puffy man, perhaps a man with weight issues. He was credible. After a little more thought, Kiera also tied a scarf at the base of his head to stop the jacket from slipping down.

They did not, however, have anything to cover his feet.

It simply wasn't possible to put an emu's feet into boots or shoes made for a human man, and then there were the giant claws to consider too.

"I don't think anyone will look at your feet," said Kiera reasonably. "It's dark, and Sonakshi and I will make sure we stay in front of you."

"Sure," Miro said, rolling his eyes, "That'll work. Hey! What are you doing?"

"Sorry Miro," said Sonakshi, bending over him with the sword *Truth Seeker*. "We can't very well go waltzing Matilda armed with a sword either. But you have very long legs. It just looked like the best place to hide it."

Miro grumbled as Sonakshi carefully slid the sword down his pant leg. "This just keeps getting better and better."

CHAPTER SEVENTEEN

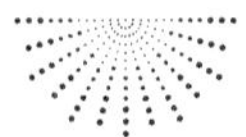

To see him is to weep. To converse with him is to stand transfixed. To be loved by him is something I cannot speak of without sounding insane. He holds my soul in his powerful hands with a touch so gentle and loving I might faint from the thought. He is life and love itself. There is no other way to describe him.
—Sonakshi's Great-Great Grandmother

They jumped off the ship onto the jetty and made their way onto land. Miro walked awkwardly in his disguise, looking also somewhat unbalanced, as if he had been drinking all afternoon. He was not used to having so much constriction about his over-stuffed, corpulent body, and he was getting very overheated, puffing and huffing in his long pants, shirt, scarf, and jacket.

Allira nervously tugged at her hat.

They were all hungry and tired, but quickly forgot this because of the excitement of being in a new country. "Look at the palm trees!" cried Allira, animated. "Oh look, that man is wearing a skirt!"

"It's not a skirt," said Kiera. "I heard it's called a *sulu,* and all the men wear them. It must be because it's so hot here.

"I can't believe I have to wear a scarf to keep this thing together." grumbled Miro. "I thought the idea was to give me camouflage, not heat stroke!"

"Sorry Miro," said Sonakshi, "it won't be for long."

Indeed, the warm night air pressed in on them, even the breeze was warm, and the air humid and smothering. But none of it at all suppressed Sonakshi, whose heart fluttered in her chest.

This was her birthplace, the place where her great-great grandfather had lived and died as a unicorn. It had also been from here that her parents had fled to save her, and now she had returned to it to save the life of another. *Or,* she thought darkly, *have I come here just for Mankini to get the better of me? Am I continuing to undo all my parents' hard work to keep me safe*? But it felt *right* to be here, and she found the heavy tropical smell of the air comforting somehow. Perhaps a part of her baby-self remembered it.

Princess Vidya's book was secured safely in her backpack, and she was truly beginning to learn what being a unicorn meant. If she could just find her great-great grandfather's book, she might actually get all the information she needed to live the life she'd always dreamed...

And she might manage to save Rowen in the process. She dearly, desperately hoped so.

The streets of Suva city were desolate that late in the night, and everything was calm and still.

Most of the buildings sat in the dark quiet of sleep, barely a soul out on the streets.

The group stopped at the first establishment they saw that had lights on, the *Lako Maieke Inn.* A small, brown-skinned man with an enormous moustache tiredly greeted them and led them into a large room. Sonakshi and Kiera took the bed as Miro insisted on roosting on the floor, and Allira said she preferred to sleep outside where the air would be fresh and cool.

She had confided in Sonakshi that hiding under the yacht during the kraken attack had been very scary for her, and she found the wide open air comforting after that.

As they went to bed, Kiera appeared agitated. She was quiet and her movements were jerky and impatient, but Sonakshi understood. She was feeling rather jittery too. Rowen was so close to them, kept captive with Mankini, and yet it felt as if they were still so far from getting to him. It was beginning to feel like an impossible task, maybe because they were all so worn down and tired. Sonakshi felt anxious and unsure now they were here.

Despite all her earlier enthusiasm, she now felt her heart sinking in her chest.

She knew that Mankini had no magical powers, yet her very name held a sort of power over Sonakshi, something she could not fully describe. Mankini had been able to kill Sonakshi's ancestor, so what type of horrible person was she? If she was capable of doing such a dark deed, what else was she capable of? Had Sonakshi under-estimated her, and would the witch bring about more deaths? They were heading into danger tomorrow, for sure, but perhaps in the light of day, their task would not seem so daunting. She really hoped so, because she almost felt that they couldn't possibly succeed.

And besides that, how would they find this book?

How would they search for it in this big place?

She had not planned this out very well. She had come here under the instruction of a ghost she wasn't even sure was real.

Sonakshi drifted into a troubled sleep, trying not to think about Rowen, surely so scared and alone all by himself. Her guilt was even greater now, knowing she had built up Keira's hopes and yet might not be able to free him after all.

* * *

The breeze brought a whisper to Sonakshi's ear, and she awoke with a start.

Sonakshi!

She sat up abruptly, checking her room left and right. Kiera was still asleep next to her and Miro was still in his corner, two conch shell earpieces on the table.

It was still dark. Crickets chirped lazily outside.

Sonakshi, come to me. Bring the sword.

It was the same voice she'd heard under the ocean yesterday.

She pushed back her blanket and crept over to the door, putting her earpiece in her pocket. If she needed help, at least she would have a way of contacting the others. She strapped the sword to her back and placed her hand on the doorknob, listening. Miro and Kiera were still fast asleep. She turned the handle slowly, and the door opened smoothly without a creak. Breathing a sigh of relief, she slipped on her shoes and stepped out into the tropical night.

It was cool breeze that tickled her cheek as she spotted Allira lying on her side under the cabin's window. She smiled at the sight, and looked down the path.

He was there. Standing there, in all his ghostly glory, was the unicorn. He stepped towards her and Sonakshi's breath caught in her throat.

You are looking for my book, child. I will show you where it is.

He turned and began down the pathway that led past the inn's entrance and, in turn, to the silent and deserted main street.

My book...

Was this her great-great grandfather?

Had the ghost of his unicorn found her in the fae forest and followed her here?

No, she had followed *him*. *His* instructions had led her to come here and not to Makogai first. A tiny part of her hesitated.

Following a ghost in the middle of night didn't seem like an idea Miro would approve of.

The unicorn, her grandfather, stopped partway down the path, and turned.

Sonakshi ambled down the path in his direction, and met him eye-to-eye.

He stood with the grace and power of a King. There was only glistening truth in that steady gaze. She knew she could trust him. He turned and began walking down the street, and she followed him at a jog.

He led her through the darkness, down the streets of the outer city and beyond, all the way into the dense jungle. Tall coconut trees swayed above her and she smelled mangoes in the air. Walking next to him, she felt something unfurl within her.

Perhaps there was something about walking next to a full-grown unicorn, even the ghost of one, that made her feel giddy on the inside. He was powerful; she could see that by his lengths of muscle rippling under that perfect coat. Even his ghostly horn glinted under the stars.

Even in death, she thought, *a unicorn is a unicorn. Magnificent.*

Her heart fluttered as she noted his grace and the way his glorious silver feathers lay confident and unassuming by his side. Would he show her how it was to fly?

They continued through the jungle and then came out onto a dirt road.

Rows of older houses sat quietly here, with peeling paint and broken shutters. Finally, he stopped outside one that was clearly deserted, with windows empty of glass and its door hanging open, half off its hinge. She followed him up the rickety wooden stairs inside.

Sonakshi shivered slightly. This house was *old,* and it was empty and eerie in here, with gigantic cobwebs decorating the sides. Her grandfather glowed even more brilliantly in the dark of the house as he stood in the back right corner. He tapped a foot on a rotten floorboard.

I met your grandmother in this house, he said. *The book is under here.*

Sonakshi hurried forward and bent on her knees, inspecting the boards as closely as she could, gently running her soft hand across the surface of the timber to feel for irregularities where there could be some kind of a hiding place. And sure enough, one side of a floorboard was slightly more elevated than the other. She placed her fingers under that side and prised it easily out, revealing a small wooden compartment beneath it.

The book sat there, its fragile and yellowed pages bound by a red cover.

She lifted it out reverently, staring at the title written in black ink, by an elegant, practiced hand. *The Way of the Unicorn.*

And underneath it was the author's name: *Ma'afu Ma'ilei.*

"This was, is your name?" she whispered, looking up at him.

He stepped back, and Sonakshi sat on the floor, slowly opening the book, caressing each page with respect, as if it held a great worth. And to Sonakshi, it did.

That is my name, yes, his voice whispered to her.

"It's a great one," she said. "Although I probably couldn't spell it."

He chuckled, a deep, resonant sound.

"You know why I'm here?" she asked, admiring the pages and pages of handwritten notes, diagrams, and pictures, that made her feel so close to her ancestor.

She knew then that she would treasure this book, and guard it for the rest of her life.

Yes, her great-great grandfather replied. *I know why you came here.*

His words came not in the form of speech, but in a whisper that was silently transmitted from his mind to her own. Yet she never hesitated in accepting these were her grandfather's words.

She began to cry, years of pent-up emotion, anger, frustration, fear, and now happiness falling out of her in the form of tears. Finally, there was someone who understood.

It's alright, my granddaughter.

Ma'afu Ma'ilei, her great-great grandfather unicorn, the first King of Macuata, lowered himself gracefully to the floorboards of his wife's childhood home.

There is much we must discuss. And there is much we need to do.

Sonakshi looked into his kind eyes and nodded, a sparkle in her gaze again.

"How are you a ghost? How are you here?" she asked, wiping her nose on her nightdress.

When a person drinks unicorn blood, her great-great grandfather said, *the immortality of the unicorn binds to that person. As the result, the unicorn is left in a state of limbo, a bewildering, in-between place. Here, he cannot die completely, but he cannot live completely either. My only comfort were the fae lands; it's a nicer place there.*

Sonakshi's heart sank at the thought of her great-great grandfather living as a ghost for a hundred years. Seeing your loved ones live and die, while not being able to talk to them... It must be terrible, an eternal torture of the soul.

"Why do did you not come to me sooner?"

No one can see me bar some of those who dwell in the fae forest. When you set your heart on coming after my murderer and then wanting to avenge my life, I was able to contact you.

"She needs to pay," Sonakshi said in a tight voice.

He blinked at her so serenely, Sonakshi swallowed a lump in her throat.

I assure you, those who steal from unicorns pay dearly for it. However, while she lives, you will never be safe. You must take great care.

Sonakshi nodded, clutching the book tightly.

I need you to do something for me, Great-Great Grandfather said.

"Anything."

Do you know what forgiveness is, my granddaughter?

She shook her head.

Forgiveness is freedom. For both the giver and the forgiven.

"How does that help me fight Mankini and save Rowen?"

The only thing that can undo a curse is forgiveness. And the forgiveness of a unicorn for a unicorn's murder will remove the spell that holds her. How old do you think Mankini is?

"Hundreds of years?"

He nodded.

And what do you think will happen to her body once we remove the curse, and she is made mortal?

"She will die," Sonakshi whispered.

He nodded his beautiful head.

This book is my life's work. Everything I know and learnt about our ways is in there. But presently, I need you only to read page three hundred and thirty-three.

Sonakshi opened the middle of the book and leafed through the pages until she found the one. When she read the title, it felt as though an icy fist held her heart.

ABSOLVING THE CURSE OF IMMORTALITY

By drinking the full life's blood of a unicorn, a person gains immortality. But a price is owed. This is the unicorn's curse.

For the matter of the reversal of a unicorn's blood curse, there is only one known way that removes the curse but preserves the immortality. The only way is to drink the full life's blood of a second unicorn.

CHAPTER EIGHTEEN

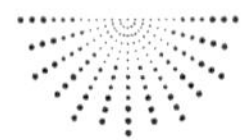

A unicorn's feathers are strength incarnate. Impenetrable, unyielding, an unending worship of the sky, of wind, of the stars.

—Ma'afu Ma'ilei, *The Way of the Unicorn, 1863.*

"Mankini has to drink *all* of my blood?" asked Sonakshi.

You must not let it come to that.

She looked at him and nodded. "I will try."

Replace the book. It is time.

Heart thumping, she did as he instructed, following him out the door and back into the night. He led her farther away from the city, uphill, where the path turned rocky.

She could smell the saltiness of the ocean again, and they hiked higher and higher. She started to pant just a little, and her grandfather slowed his pace to allow her to catch her breath.

Up and up they went, following a trail that led through tropical trees. When they emerged through the forest, finally, Sonakshi found them at the edge of a spectacular cliff, the dark swirling ocean beneath them. Fear spiked within her. Did he mean her to fly?

He nodded his head towards the horizon.

Makogai lies a short flight north.

Sonakshi stepped backwards, sweat trickling down her spine. "I- I cannot."

He turned and considered her, and then slowly, in a measured way, walked around her in a slow circle.

Close your eyes, child.

Reluctantly, she did. The cool night air swept against her face. She could hear her blood pumping in her head after that walk, and her feet and her hands were buzzing.

Listen to the night.

Leaves rustled in trees high above her, the waves crashed beneath her, and her heart pounded within her.

A unicorn knows no fear. And you are a unicorn as strong and as brave as any. And then, *Listen deeper into the night, child.*

Sonakshi screwed her eyes tight and concentrated, but heard nothing different.

There you stand upon the threshold of fear. Everything you've ever been afraid of stands in that fortress. Your enemy, death, failure. What will you do?

What does it mean to be a unicorn?

Let go of your fear and you will find out.

She took a deep breath and relaxed her shoulders.

Let go of the fearful girl child. Embrace the fearless unicorn. Claim your birthright. I am here with you. I am watching over you. You have no use for fear.

Sonakshi listened to her great-great grandfather's wise and reassuring words. She was his granddaughter, and she could confirm there was no fear in his voice. Only powerful, pure, grace. *Even in death, a unicorn is a unicorn,* she thought. *And I am a unicorn as strong as any.*

She thought of her parents and let go her need to run.

She thought of the Yowie and let go her need to hide.

She thought of Kiera and found strength.

She thought of Rowen and found confidence.

She felt the stars twinkling above her in the night sky and found wonder. She felt the mighty strength of the waves crashing below and felt its grace within her. She felt the rush of the wind—and something wondrous unfurled within her gut.

Sonakshi flashed into her unicorn form and felt as if the trees and the waves and the water each breathed a huge sigh of relief. She felt her horn glimmer under the moon and she felt her wings, every feather, every muscle, as she never had before. She was also amazed to feel that *Truth Seeker* had remained strapped to her back; the straps had lengthened, with some sort of mermaid magic, as she changed shape.

The wind caressed her fondly as she turned to meet the gaze of her ancestor again.

There, he whispered. *Even to unicorns, a foal is a wondrous thing. You have it, I see it now.*

He turned to his left, gazing into the jungle. *We are not alone, child.*

Sonakshi felt her before she saw her. Allira came bounding through the bushland at a rapid pace. Sonakshi stepped backwards as Allira burst from the bushes in a shower of leaves and dust, skidding to a halt in front of her.

"Sona! You can't go!"

Allira panted and there were tears in her eyes. Sonakshi could feel her friend's fear, her worry, and her need to protect her.

"You can't just go, Sona; she'll kill you!"

Sonakshi smiled at her friend. "I know."

"Oh. I… I smelled your scent on the wind and followed you here."

"You're good at that. Following me."

Sonakshi laughed at Allira's guilty face. "I'm just teasing you, my friend."

"Please, wait for the others—"

"This is my fight, Allira. Mankini is my duty. A unicorn must be the one to do this."

"But we all came with—"

"I know. And I love you for it. But it's time for me to claim my birthright."

"I—"

"I need you go to back to bed. Stay with the others."

"But—"

"*Please,* Allira. I'm telling you, my friend."

Allira bowed her head.

"I have to go now. Go on, go back to the others."

Allira gave Sonakshi one last uncertain look and slowly turned away.

Sonakshi turned back to her grandfather. He tossed his head in happiness, his mane shining brilliantly. And he galloped towards the cliff face, and with a powerful sweep of his wings, he was in the air. His ghostly body shone in the night sky and he flew in a wide arc, circling back towards her. He hovered in the sky, watching over her, just as he had promised.

Sonakshi took a deep breath and exhaled. She cantered towards the cliff's edge and extended out her wings. The night air sang to her, and she swooped her wings down once, twice, and her hooves left the grass. She flapped her wings and as she soared into the stars, her heart was lifted with her. She rose into the sky, swooping her wings again and again. It felt so natural, so right, so wonderful. It took almost no effort at all, and before she knew it, she was incredibly high in the sky. She looked below, saw the ocean beneath her and she could feel it laughing at her. They were alike now, her and sea. Both knew who they were.

The feeling of flight was incredible.

How could she not have known how to do this before? Before... when she was frightened. There was nothing but joy within her now, not a trace of fear.

As she rose to meet her grandfather, she was breathless with delight. She could feel his approval emanating from him like the fragrance of a flower.

There was work to be done.

Follow me to Makogai.

CHAPTER NINETEEN

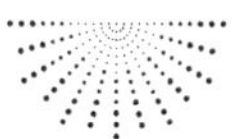

There are some things only a unicorn knows. The sound of spring flowers blooming, the smell of midnight after winter rain, the touch of moonlight upon summer's still water, and the sight of a heart breaking when it learns the truth.
—Ma'afu Ma'ilei, *The Way of the Unicorn, 1863.*

They flew high over the midnight-coloured ocean, close together, great-great grandfather and granddaughter, both relishing the rush of wind against their faces. Sonakshi viewed the sky with interest. The world seemed so different from up this high. Serene, and stunning.

Here, the air was thinner and colder, and the stars even more beautiful.

The sea still stretched on forever, but her waves just seemed less threatening. The character of the wind changed under her wings, and she felt the minute shifts through the movement of her feathers, and adjusted how she flew depending on the course of the wind.

She quickly learned how to veer left and right, as well as to swoop downwards. She followed the lead of her grandfather, who looked at her fondly when she copied him exactly.

Soon, Makogai came into view, a small all green island, sitting innocently in the water.

Rowen is there, Sonakshi thought. *Hold on, Rowen, please be okay.*

They descended, and as they did so, Sonakshi leaned forward and pointed her wings backwards, allowing gravity to take her lower. They wheeled in circles around the island, descending with each wheel. Her grandfather led her towards the north side of the island where she could see a black circle, the top of a dark tower.

They headed towards the trees and grandfather found a little runway for her to land on.

She descended towards the strip of land and let her hooves skim the tall grass, sweeping her wings forward to slow her down. The bushes in front of her swayed from the wind that her wings blasted at them as her hooves touched down on the wild grass.

She blew air from her chest, reeling from her incredible first flight, but the sight of black stone among the trees sobered her mind, making her think of the task at hand.

She followed the ghostly form in front of her and they emerged into a clearing where the black fortress towered ominously into the sky.

Sonakshi went to move forward to find the entrance, but her grandfather was still.

When I am gone, Sonakshi, you must promise me two things.

"Anything, Grandfather."

Read my entire book. You must know everything about unicorns. And...do not forget me.

"How could I ever forget you?" Sonakshi whispered. "You have given me so much."

Walking around the perimeter of the fortress, they came to large double doors made of solid wood. Two men sat at a table by the door, eating flat round bread and some type of curry. Sonakshi exhaled deeply. *Rowen, I'm here for you. Please, hang in there. I'm coming.*

The one facing Sonakshi choked on his curry and pointed at her.

His companion turned to look at her and dropped his food, his mouth gaping open.

They both stood and continued to stare at her, wide-eyed.

She cleared her throat and spoke clearly.

"I have come to see Mankini."

They stared at her for a moment longer before the one closest to her visibly shook himself and nodded, gesturing towards the door.

The other knocked on the wide door next to him, three times.

She moved around them in a wide arc and their eyes followed her about the room, but they did not move an inch. She noticed that both of them were armed with knives and what looked like a machete—

flat, short, wide sort of sword rested vertically against the stone wall.

She waited in front of the door.

After a few long moments, a little window at the top of the door opened. Two beady black eyes in a brown furry head widened in surprise.

"Hello Batuman," she said. "I have come as asked."

He disappeared, and after a moment, the door pulled open with an enormous creak, as if it was not often used. After a moment, it seemed that Batuman could not open it any further so Sonakshi gave it a hefty shove with her shoulder.

Batuman stood on the large stone steps leading upwards. He stared at her open-mouthed and did not say anything. Sonakshi thought her grandfather would not approve of her giving him a good thumping right now, so she ignored him and went up the stairs.

After a couple of seconds, climbing up the stairs, she came to a landing that opened up to a large room. She saw a window and a chair with its back to her.

"Who was it, Batuman?" croaked a voice from the chair.

Sonakshi rounded the corner and saw the room in full view. On one side sat a kitchenette and next to it, in a cage against the wall on the far side, sat a boy with flaming red hair. He blinked his green eyes, once, twice.

"Princess Sona?" he said with surprise. She nodded, her eyes suddenly teary. Her great-great grandfather came to stand by his cage, as if he did not want the little boy to stand alone.

Mankini's chair creaked loudly as Sonakshi stepped into the room and the face of Sonakshi's nightmares came into view. Sonakshi's heart skipped a beat as Mankini slowly came from around the chair to stand in front of her. She was unmistakable.

Hunched, with one evil eye glittering, her mouth twisted into a smirk.

"Well, well, well," she croaked. "You came to save your friend after all. But it took you long enough"

"No, Sona! Get away from here! Run!" cried Rowen, gripping the bars tightly.

Sonakshi exhaled slowly, calming herself. "It's alright, Rowen."

She looked at Mankini. "Yes, I'm sure your spy told you I was coming."

"Figured that out, did you?"

"Let Rowen go. He's just a child, for God's sake."

"Not until I am given what I am owed."

"Owed?"

"Yes. Your ancestor did this to me, and now *you* will fix it."

"You did this to yourself, Mankini, you can't blame anyone else."

Mankini jeered at her. "Do you know what a unicorn is?" she said nastily.

Sonakshi frowned.

"A unicorn is a sacrificial animal, made for humans to use as they please. That is what you are. Nothing more than a creature made to serve *me. To be sacrificed for me."*

"That's not true and you know it!" said Sonakshi,

anger rising within her. "You are dark and twisted, and that's why you look the way you do!"

Mankini screamed on the spot. "You! You and your kind *did this to me!*"

Sonakshi felt a small movement by her feet as Batuman waddled into the room. As she turned to glance at him, Batuman rose into the air and threw something at her.

Rowen gave a cry of warning.

Sonakshi made to move, but it was too late. A black, glittering rope encircled itself around her throat and settled there like a necklace.

"No!" cried Rowen.

Mankini cackled with laugher. "It is *done!*"

Sonakshi went to rear in annoyance but found she couldn't move. The necklace had somehow paralysed her into position. She panicked, heart pounding fast.

"Well done, Batuman," said Mankini with approval. "Boy, be quiet or I will tape your mouth closed!" Rowen whimpered and pressed his face against the bars of the cage.

Sonakshi felt Batuman moving around her hooves but could not look down to see what he was doing. She tugged against her feet, but they would not move.

She tried to move her head, but that too was stuck in place.

"You all thought I was powerless," Mankini snarled, "since the curse took hold of me."

Sonakshi glanced at her grandfather.

If she just said the words, would that be enough to end Mankini?

It won't be enough to just say the words, Sonakshi. You must mean it. You must feel the forgiveness within you.

Sonakshi looked at Mankini and felt nothing positive within her.

She *hated* Mankini. She wanted her to pay for what she had done. How could she stand there, knowing that she was a murderer?

"You see, Sonakshi," Mankini continued, stepping closer. "I spent my *life* researching how to capture and contain unicorns. I may not have any magic now, but I have many magical objects that have my old magic still in them. Inventions of my own crafting."

Batuman waddled over to Mankini, holding something large in his claws.

It was a clear jug, almost the same size as himself.

He held it up to Mankini, and she bent with a groan, taking it from him.

"Unicorns exist to sacrifice themselves for human kind. Congratulations, Princess," she said mockingly. "You are fulfilling what you were born for."

"You won't get away with this!" said Sonakshi angrily, but she was surprised she could move her mouth to talk.

But Mankini wasn't listening; she was squinting at Sonakshi's back.

"What is that, Batuman? Get it off her."

Batuman flew up clumsily and came to sit on Sonakshi's back.

"It looks like a sword, Madam!"

She could feel him fiddling with the straps, unbuckling them. Mankini shuffled closer, placing the large jug on a stool a short distance away where they could all see it.

"Your blood will remove this curse from me," she said gently. "It will free me back into the life I deserve."

Sonakshi tried to tug her legs again, but they were still stuck in place.

"Don't bother trying to escape," said Mankini. "These very shackles held your great-great grandfather." She tapped the jug next to her. "And this very jug held your grandfather's blood. And now, it will hold yours too. I can probably fill it to the very top, and bleed you dry, dear."

Batuman shuffled on her back, and Sonakshi felt *Truth Seeker* slide off her back and clatter to the floor.

"All I have to do," Mankini said, ignoring him, "Is activate the spell and your blood will pour from you…." She pointed at Sonakshi. "…into here directly." She pointed at the jug. "Such is my genius."

Sonakshi stared at the jug in horror. It would be that easy? Sonakshi's grandfather cantered around the room. *Feel it, Sonakshi, then say the words.* She wanted to shake her head. She couldn't! She did not forgive Mankini. She just didn't, and probably never would.

Mankini walked over to Sonakshi and she wanted to cringe away from the disfigured woman. Up close, she looked even more terrifying. Her face was lined with so many wrinkles, and she smelled *bad,* like the compost bin her mother had set up back home, but worse.

But Sonakshi couldn't even wrinkle her nose.

She just stared at Mankini's face as she came to

stand right in front of her. Mankini extended a long crooked finger towards her neck and Sonakshi couldn't help but close her eyes.

Being so close to this murderer made her want to throw up and cry at the same time.

She couldn't do as her grandfather asked, she just couldn't.

How could this vile, repulsive and cruel hag ever receive forgiveness?

She felt a pressure in her neck as Mankini pressed something on the necklace there, activating it. Immediately, Sonakshi felt a strange, tugging sensation from deep within her. The magic was drawing out her own, her very life force. She opened her eyes just as Mankini laughed with delight, staring at the jug. Sonakshi looked over and saw that at the bottom of the jug was a swirling silvery substance, filling the jug seemingly out of nowhere.

My blood, Sonakshi thought, *that's actually my blood.*

Sonakshi realised with a jolt that she had never actually seen her own blood.

She had never bled, as her skin was tough.

Even in a fall, or by some accident, her skin had never broken and bled on its own.

"Unicorn blood has such a lovely colour, doesn't it?" Mankini said, smiling at the slowly filling jug. "In just short of ten minutes, I'm sure it'll be full. And I'll tell you..." she whispered. "It tastes wonderful." She spun around happily. "Oh Batuman! I can feel it already! I'm going to be so happy!"

Sonakshi heard Rowen sobbing quietly from the cage.

Batuman clapped and danced, and Sonakshi felt a little light-headed.

It couldn't end this way, it just couldn't.

"Now, let's have a look at this, shall we?" Mankini said, eyeing *Truth Seeker* on the floor.

Batuman waddled over to it and pulled the hilt of it upwards, angling it towards her.

Mankini took the sword, weighing it in her hands, impressed.

"This is—" She frowned deeply and inhaled sharply, looking up at Sonakshi in surprise.

Sonakshi looked into Mankini's eyes and saw the truth reveal itself in the depths of her pupils. Mankini's eyes bored into her with a mixture of shock and anger, and an instant felt like eternity. Inside Mankini was a frightened little girl who had been broken and hurt.

Life had struck her down and Mankini had responded with anger, hate, and jealousy.

She had let all her pain and fear stew within her, and like a pot boiling over, it had come to a head when she decided that power was the most important thing in her life.

She had sought only to rule above the father who had hurt her, the mother who had never loved her, and the husband who had envied her. Pain had grown into fear, which had become anger, an anger so fierce it poisoned her heart. She had wanted love and, in time, she discarded that as hopeless and chose the dark path instead. The dark path was the easy route, the one that would never abandon her, never use and abuse her, never leave her alone, and broken.

The dark path was the one that took from others what it wanted.

And for a change, others were the ones who would be left broken and hurt.

Then, Mankini had wanted a life that could not be taken from her, and so she had chosen immortality, and she chose to take it the way she knew best, by force.

So, she hunted down Ma'afu Ma'ilei, a King of Macuata, and executed a plan she had devised over ten years. And then, of course, she took his life.

Sonakshi saw all of this in the space of a heartbeat, and her heart knew the truth of things, swelling inside of her.

Mankini dropped the sword and glared at it with distaste.

"Mankini." Sonakshi's voice was strangely deep, for it was full of the weight of what she was about to do. Mankini scowled at her.

Sonakshi took in a great breath, preparing herself for what she was about to do.

And she stepped forward, looking Mankini in her eyes.

"I forgive you," Sonakshi said, at first under her breath as if they were words she dared not say. But then she mustered her strength and said it again, louder. "I forgive you, Mankini."

Mankini's nostrils flared, and she opened her mouth to speak.

But she stopped herself. Her eyes widened.

"No," she croaked. "No, no, no, no, no, no, *no!*"

There was disbelief in her voice, and then it grew into fear.

"What have you done!" Mankini clutched her stomach and doubled over in pain.

She gasped and reached for the floor.

"Mistress!" Batuman screamed, rushing over, grasping at her face.

But he could do nothing for his mistress.

Her grandfather tossed his head and reared mightily. *"Thank you, Granddaughter, I am finally at rest...."*

His image faded into nothingness.

Sonakshi smiled at the empty space, her eyes burning with hot tears.

"I understand why you did it, Mankini. I understand you pursued me. But you will pursue me no longer."

"There are others," she wheezed from the floor. "There will always be others."

Sonakshi remained serene. No fear spiked within her.

"Perhaps. But they will have no power over me now."

Mankini wheezed.

"Goodbye, Mankini."

Gold unicorn light flooded around Mankini, and Batuman yelped and jumped backwards. When it faded, there was only Mankini's black dress with a long pile of grey dust on the spot where the hag had lain. "Madam!" Batuman sobbed and lurched onto the dress, clutching it to his heart. "Where did you go? Where are you?"

"Her immortality was taken away, Batuman. She has passed on."

Sonakshi felt her vision go blurry.

She looked at the glass jug and saw that it was almost half full of silver, glowing blood.

"Princess!" cried Rowen, standing powerless in his cage. "Batuman! Let me out!"

"Rowen," Sonakshi said weakly, "I'm sorry, I—"

She felt very drowsy suddenly and felt her eyelids grow heavy. Too much blood had been taken from her

She fought to keep them open, but this was a battle she could not fight alone.

Somewhere very far away, she could hear shouting. Rowen must have been calling for her. She tried to focus on it but suddenly, there was a loud crash, and everything went black.

CHAPTER TWENTY

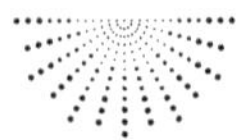

More powerful than the blood of the unicorn are her tears, which give the power of a unicorn to any who consume it.
—Ma'afu Ma'ilei, *The Way of the Unicorn, 1863.*

Allira raced back from the cliff to the Lako Maieke.

She dodged fallen trees and leapt over them, sending a mongoose scattering as her heart pounded. She just couldn't let Sonakshi go alone to Makogai, she just couldn't!

She knew that Sonakshi thought she could do this on her own, but unicorn or no, it was simply way too dangerous. But something had changed in Sonakshi lately; Allira knew it by the glitter of knowledge she had seen in Sonakshi's eyes, and in the confident way she stood.

And Allira had watched Sonakshi leap into the air

and fly off with such ease that she could only stare in awe. But Allira had quickly realised what it all meant.

If Sonakshi's great-great grandfather had fallen to Mankini, then she knew her unicorn friend would need backup. Luckily, she'd taken the conch-shell earpiece Princess Meera had given them. That would serve them well now.

"Wake up you two!" she cried.

There was no reply.

"Miro! Kiera! Wake up!" cried Allira.

There was a shuffling noise and Allira heard Kiera's voice very far away from her own earpiece. "Did anyone hear that?"

"Kiera!" Allira cried again. "Miro, wake up! Where's Sona?"

And then there came more shuffling as the earpiece shifted and Kiera's voice was crystal clear, as if she were running right next to Allira.

"Hello?"

"Kiera, it's me."

"Who?"

"Allira, you dingbat! Sona has gone to Makogai by herself."

"What?"

"Get dressed. I'm coming, and we'll go to the *Dimple* to sail across and meet her there."

"Copy that, Allira; we're ready."

Within minutes, Allira arrived back at their room where Miro and Kiera were standing ready. "Let's go!" said Kiera.

They all ran back out of the inn as Allira filled them in on what she'd keen.

"She really flew?" asked Kiera between huffs of air.

"I saw it with my own eyes."

Miro and Allira, being much faster than Kiera on her two human legs, spurred her on, reducing their own speed so she could keep up.

They ran through the dark streets of Suva city and eventually came to the harbour. As they passed through the line of yachts and ships and the purple sails of the *Dimple* came into view, Allira's heart leapt into her mouth.

She could see two people bending over and inspecting the boat.

"Who's that?" she turned and asked the others.

Kiera squinted and shook her head.

They pounded down the jetty anxiously and then Kiera gave an almighty cry.

"Your Majesties!"

Allira and Miro exchanged a look of shock as they slowed down and could see the two adults properly. Kiera did not slow down, however, and ran straight into the arms of the woman. With wide brown eyes and honey coloured skin, Sonakshi's resemblance to her mother was unmistakable. The man who must have been Sonakshi's father stood next to her.

He lifted his coal black eyes from Kiera to Allira, and then to Miro, and he looked at them thoughtfully, rubbing his chin.

"What are you doing here?" sobbed Kiera.

"Captain Sampson sent us a message about Rowen

being kidnapped by Mankini, and then King Farrion told us you had visited his palace. They loaned us their fastest boat to come here. Where is she? Where is my daughter?"

"That's precisely why we're here," said Allira quickly.

If either the King or Queen thought it strange that Allira was talking, it did not show on their faces.

"Sonakshi snuck out in the middle of the night to go there by herself."

Queen Ria turned to King Devin in panic. "We have to stop her."

A voice came from nowhere, surrounding them, wrapping them in a deep, solemn baritone.

Sonakshi is in danger. Go to Mankini's fortress immediately. Cut the necklace.

They exchanged wide-eyed looks for half a second before they jumped into action.

Kiera leaped into the *Dimple,* holding it open for the King and Queen. Miro and Allira bounded on as Kiera scurried to the helm of the boat.

"Dimple! Take us to Makogai as fast as you can!"

The sails billowed and the *Dimple* immediately manoeuvred out of the bay; they all fell into their seats as she charged out, into the open nighttime sea.

Makogai came into view impossibly quickly and above the canopy of the trees, a tall fortress stood, imposing and dark. But the *Dimple* slowed down as it approached the island, and then stopped completely with a good half a kilometer of water still between them.

"Why did it stop?" asked Kiera, standing.

The King stood and pointed to the ocean.

"There's a reef here. The *Dimple* cannot get any closer."

As if the boat understood their words, a small splash came from the side. They looked over the edge and saw a yellow lifeboat complete with two oars inflating itself in the water.

King Devin laughed and helped Kiera and Ria climb down.

Then he looked at Miro and Allira expectantly.

"No fear, Your Majesty," said Miro, coming forward. "I have a healthy pair of legs."

And they watched in shock as Miro jumped straight from the *Dimple* into the lifeboat.

"Argh!" cried Kiera, clutching to the side of the boat as it jumped and swayed violently.

Queen Ria laughed as Miro settled himself in the boat while Kiera looked ready to have a fit. Allira took a softer approach, awkwardly using the ladder on the side of the *Dimple* to help her. King Devin stepped lightly onto the boat and they began to ready themselves to take the oars. But the lifeboat, animated by the same magic as the *Dimple,* blasted forward through the reef, as its five occupants clutched onto the handholds for dear life.

The lifeboat pushed itself onto a beach, and without a word, they climbed out of it, Allira and Miro speeding into the bushes and leaving the humans to run along behind them.

They arrived at Mankini's fortress within minutes,

finding two alarmed men holding large, sharp weapons, ready to fight.

"There are guards here, Kiera!" Miro said into his earpiece, "Be careful!"

Allira wasted no time and bounded forward, kicking one man aside, while Miro charged at the other. Both men screamed and fell. Allira and Miro snatched their weapons from them with beak and paw, holding the men in place.

King Devin charged into the clearing, taking the scene in, and began unravelling the ropes he had brought. He gave one length to Allira. "Tie him up!" he called out, and helped Miro tie up the other. The men growled angrily, but Miro gave each one of them a sharp tap with his beak and they quietened immediately.

Kiera and Queen Ria arrived next, panting. Kiera immediately pushed the large door open and bolted up the stairs before anyone could stop her, yelling Rowen's name.

Batuman appeared in the doorway, flying in a wobbly way, and Allira shot past King Devin and jumped into the air, snatching him mid-flight and tackling him to the ground. He yelled out in shock and protest.

"I got my tail back, you evil—"

"Mankini is gone!" he squealed thickly, and Allira stilled in shock.

The King and Queen bolted into the tower after Kiera as Miro, holding another length of rope in his beak, offered it to Allira.

Kiera rushed into the room and viewed the scene, panting. Rowen stood in the corner sobbing behind the bars of a cage. She ran towards him, but he shook his head, jumping up and down desperately.

"No! No! Go to Sona!"

Kiera looked at where he was pointing and saw Sonakshi standing stationary opposite the kitchen. "Oh no, Sona," cried Kiera, rushing over to her.

"That's her blood!" cried Rowen, and Kiera spotted the jug full of silver liquid. "Cut the necklace, quickly!"

Kiera snatched a knife from the kitchen bench in the corner. She held the necklace in one shaking hand and sawed through it with the other. As soon as the dark beads dropped away, Sonakshi crumpled to the floor.

"No!" Kiera fell to the floor now too. She hugged Sonakshi around the neck and sobbed, tears streaming down her face in a waterfall. "Please don't die from this."

"Grandfather?"

"It's Kiera,"

"Kiera," whispered Sonakshi. "I did it, but somehow, I still—"

"Shh, don't." Kiera pressed her face against Sonakshi's neck. "You saved Rowen, and you can't die now, you just can't."

The face of her parents swam in her vision as the King and Queen entered the room.

"Sonakshi," her mother whispered with such pain that Sonakshi wanted to speak, but she couldn't manage it.

"You shouldn't have come here, my child," whispered her father, running over and pulling her into his arms. Her mother sat next to them, clutching at Sonakshi's face.

Kiera wailed loudly and clutched on to Sonakshi, burying her face into Sonakshi's mane.

Miro and Allira arrived with a tied-up Batuman. Allira threw Batuman onto the floor and grabbed a set of keys from a hook on the wall, setting Rowen free.

Rowen stared at her and Miro before running over to Sonakshi and the group on the floor. Allira and Miro gathered around their friends, at a loss for words.

"No," Rowen whispered. Kiera lifted her head and put her arm around her little brother.

"I'm glad you're okay, little frog,"

He huddled into her, tears streaming down his face.

Queen Ria patted Rowen's cheek, smiling sadly at him.

All at once, Sonakshi's entire body erupted with light and all those watching gasped. Kiera and Rowen jumped back in shock.

Sonakshi felt a powerful sensation within her body. Something in her was pulling and tugging, drawing something in.

Miro gasped and pointed to the jug on the table next to them. The silver liquid was disappearing, its level lowering by the second.

Sonakshi groaned as she felt her blood return to her. The jug now stood empty.

She felt a burst of energy and yelped in surprise.

The light faded, and she saw the stunned faces of her parents, Kiera, and the others, as clear as day.

Kiera screamed and hugged Sonakshi, while her parents exchanged looks of shock.

"What just happened?" Kiera cried, rubbing her eyes.

King Devin cuddled Sonakshi, stroking her mane, looking into her eyes.

Queen Ria looked from Sonakshi to Kiera and back to Sonakshi. Quickly, she put two and two together. "Kiera, did you ever swallow one of Sona's tears?" she asked.

"What—no, of course not!" said Sonakshi, affronted.

"Yes," said Kiera, smiling at her friend. "But I did. Sona, you cried all over me, remember? After the mermaids saved us. I told you I swallowed one by accident!"

"That's what's done it. Kiera, *you* just saved Sona."

Kiera gaped like a fish. "I have powers?"

"How did Kiera swallowing a unicorn tear help just now?" asked Sonakshi.

"Those who consume unicorn tears obtain the powers of a unicorn for a short period," her mother explained, grinning from ear to ear. "By taking in Sona's tears, Kiera then pressed her forehead against her, and like a unicorn horn, it healed her!"

Sonakshi flashed back into her human form so she could hug both her parents in one go.

"How did you get here?"

"We figured it out," said the Queen. "We found a few letters in your room and then spoke with Princess Vidya after her father notified us you went to his palace."

She shook her head ruefully. "You sure know how to give us a scare, Sona."

"Allira woke us all up," said Miro, "and we ran into your parents by the *Dimple.*"

"Can we get out of here, please?" piped Rowen. "And can you tell me about your friends?" He peeped shyly under his lashes at Miro and Allira.

Sonakshi and Kiera looked at each other and burst into laughter. Kiera swooped up Rowen and swung him about the room. She set him down, still laughing, "Gosh, Rowen, you smell bad! But yes, I guess we've been around these two for so long we forgot that talking emus and kangaroos are kind of new for others!"

As Miro allowed Rowen to touch his wing, Sonakshi went over to *Truth Seeker* still lying next to Mankini's clothes, and picked it up.

"Kiera told us where you got that from," said her father softly, his hand around her shoulder. "We should return it to the King under the sea."

Sonakshi looked up at him and smiled, "It saved the day, really."

"No," he sighed, "I think you did that, with Kiera and your friends."

The King and Queen led the troupe out of Mankini's tower.

He pulled the men outside onto their feet and

prodded them, as they all walked through the forest, Batuman safely in Allira's custody.

They all climbed on to the *Dimple* and her father led their two hostages into the cabin below.

Allira refused to let go of Batuman, so King Devin shrugged and sat next to them, smiling at Sonakshi.

The sun was rising in the east and Sonakshi felt rather inspired. She grinned at her parents and flashed into her unicorn self, and jumped into the air, flapping her swings. Her mother cried out in shock as Sonakshi rose effortlessly into the sky, her eye on the orange glow of the sun on the horizon. Kiera jumped up and down, cheering her, arms raised high in the air. Sonakshi rose into the sky and wheeled.

Her parents stared at her, jaws slack.

She felt the rush of air under her wings, and it felt so wonderful she swooped playfully and wheeled in a circle around the boat. She looked at her father and a slow joyous smile spread over his lips. Her mother had her hands clasped against her chest and her tears glistened in the dawn light.

They were never scared of me, Sonakshi thought, *They were just scared* for *me.*

EPILOGUE

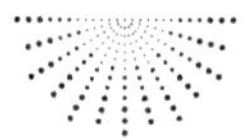

There are few in the world whom the unicorn consider their noble companions. First are the fae who share the knowledge of the sky and all things wise and fair. Second are the merpeople who share the knowledge of the water and all things noble and true. And third are the pure of heart who can only share their love, the most valuable thing of all.
—Ma'afu Ma'ilei, *The Way of the Unicorn, 1863.*

A little over a week later, Sonakshi sat on the beach of Denarau, just a little way off Fiji's main island. The sun shone pleasantly down on their little group of seven. Sonakshi, Kiera and Rowen were building a sandcastle, complete with miniature versions of themselves. Sonakshi's parents, along with the Lord and Lady of Cabbage Tree Creek, Kiera's parents, were slathered in bright white zinc and sunscreen next to them, chatting.

On the day of Rowen's release, Sonakshi's parents were met ashore by the Fijian Police, Captain Sampson and the Lord and Lady of Cabbage Tree Creek. They handed over the two human servants of Mankini to be put into jail, along with a very annoyed Batuman, and Rowen was swamped by his parents and promptly taken to be fed and bathed thoroughly.

They advised the Fijian police that if they went to Makogai fortress, they would find it now empty. The police had exchanged knowing looks. Everyone had known about the 'cursed witch' living there, so no one had ever approached the place.

Miro and Allira had bid them goodbye the next day, taking the *Dimple* back to Freshwater Bay to return to their families, with promises of a visit to Sonakshi's home in the Blue Mountains. King Farrion, Vidya's father, met them ashore, to guide them safely back, away from Yowies and the like, something for which Miro was very grateful.

And so they recovered in Suva for a little while, Sonakshi reading the two books she had acquired with Kiera, and her parents taking notes to learn every possible thing about her.

Queen Ria had cried upon first receiving her great grandfather's handwritten words and asked over and over that Sonakshi describe his ghost, 'just one more time'.

Her parents visited their family home in Labasa, visiting with friends and family who all still lived there. Sonakshi's grandparents had passed on, but some of their family had been in on the secret of the unicorn and looked at her golden eyes knowingly.

They had then taken the opportunity to teach Sonakshi about where she was born, touring around, and showing her and Kiera the sugarcane fields and the spectacular gardens and beaches of the tropical islands that made up Fiji.

It was their last day there before they returned to the Blue Mountains. Sonakshi had promised not to change into unicorn form or fly in the presence of unsuspecting civilians, and she no longer flashed into unicorn form by accident when she got a fright.

"Does this mean we'll get out more?" she had asked her mother one night.

"I don't see why not," she answered, stroking her hair. "Mankini is not an issue anymore and if something else comes along, I know we can deal with it together."

Sonakshi had whooped with joy and Kiera had begun to plan when they could next go to her ancestral home in Ireland where, she supposed, should be even more fae and other fantastical creatures.

"Will you forgive me, Sona?" asked her mother, gazing at her. "For keeping you secret and fearful, cooped up in our castle?"

Sonakshi smiled, "How could I not?"

AFTERWORD

I hope you enjoyed this story. The next book, *The Fae Princess* (Princess Vidya's story), will be out in January 2021, so keep an eye out for it.

If you would like to sign up to my newsletter and be notified of updates check out www.pacificprincess.com

Lastly, if you enjoyed *The Unicorn Princess,* please leave a review online. It's the single best way to support your favourite authors.

ACKNOWLEDGMENTS

Thank you to my inspiration my beautiful niece, Sonakshi, without whom this book would never have been written. If she had not asked me to write her a story about unicorns, I never would have attempted a middle grade novel!

Thank you to Mum, Rachna and Rishta for your beta reading and words of wisdom.

Thank you to my copy editor Annie Jenkinson who has given me a lot of valuable insight into this manuscript.

And a heartfelt thanks to the cover illustrator Adrian, who took my breath away with his spectacular artwork.

ABOUT THE AUTHOR

Ektaa Bali is an emerging author of middle grade, young adult and adult fantasy fiction. She enjoys cuddling with her puppy Toby and baking with unusual ingredients. This is her first middle grade novel.

Printed in Great Britain
by Amazon